"I'll be fine."

Destiny could see that Logan was waiting for her to convince him. "I don't have any other choice. Paula's killer is out there somewhere and I intend to catch him. I can't do that if I fall apart."

"No, you can't," he agreed. "But if you need someone to talk to—or not talk to," he added with a smile that was beginning to weave its way under her skin even though she was doing her best to ignore it, "I'm available."

"You're a good guy, Logan Cavanaugh," she told him quietly just before she impulsively brushed her lips against his cheek.

Logan felt something within his gut tighten so quickly and so hard, for a second it was difficult for him to draw in a breathe.

Every fiber of his being wanted to pull her into his arms and to kiss her back. The right way. And he had a strong feeling that he wouldn't get any resistance from her.

But that would be taking unfair advantage of her vulnerable state. Their time would come—he was fairly certain of that. But not tonight.

Dear Reader,

You are holding in your hands the latest book in the Cavanaugh Justice series. Logan Cavanaugh is another one of Sean Cavanaugh's (a.k.a Cavelli) sons. A free spirit who takes just about everything in stride, Logan finds his laid-back attitude challenged when he is temporarily paired with Destiny Richardson, his father's chief assistant in the crime lab. She also just happens to be the sister of what appears to be a serial killer's latest victim.

The latter designation has yet to come to light since the murders are all staged to appear like suicides—except that Destiny is positive that her younger sister would have never committed suicide, and she is prepared to go to hell and back to prove it. Logan, the primary investigative detective on what started out as an open-and-shut case, has no choice but to follow Destiny in order to keep her safe. But who is going to keep each of them safe from one another?

I hope you enjoy this latest installment. As ever, I thank you for reading and from the bottom of my heart I wish you someone to love who loves you back.

Marie Ferrarella

MARIE FERRARELLA

Cavanaugh's Surrender

23

HARLEQUIN®
entertain, enrich, inspire™

Recycling programs
for this product may
not exist in your area.

ISBN-13: 978-0-373-27795-7

CAVANAUGH'S SURRENDER

Books by Marie Ferrarella

Harlequin Romantic Suspense

Private Justice #1664
***The Doctor's Guardian* #1675
**A Cavanaugh Christmas* #1683
Special Agent's Perfect Cover #1688
**Cavanaugh's Bodyguard* #1699
*Cavanaugh Rules #1715
**Cavanaugh's Surrender* #1725

Loving the Right Brother #1977
The 39-Year-Old Virgin #1983
****A Lawman for Christmas* #2006
††*Prescription for Romance* #2017
†††*Doctoring the Single Dad* #2031
†††*Fixed Up with Mr. Right?* #2041
†††*Finding Happily-Ever-After* #2060
†††*Unwrapping the Playboy* #2084
‡*Fortune's Just Desserts* #2107

Silhouette Romantic Suspense

***A Doctor's Secret* #1503
***Secret Agent Affair* #1511
**Protecting His Witness* #1515
Colton's Secret Service #1528
The Heiress's 2-Week Affair #1556
*Cavanaugh Pride #1571
**Becoming a Cavanaugh* #1575
The Agent's Secret Baby #1580
**The Cavanaugh Code* #1587
**In Bed with the Badge* #1596
**Cavanaugh Judgment* #1612
Colton by Marriage #1616
**Cavanaugh Reunion* #1623
***In His Protective Custody* #1644

Harlequin American Romance

Pocketful of Rainbows #145
‡‡*The Sheriff's Christmas Surprise* #1329
‡‡*Ramona and the Renegade* #1338
‡‡*The Doctor's Forever Family* #1346
Montana Sheriff #1369
Holiday in a Stetson #1378
   "The Sheriff Who Found Christmas"
‡‡*Lassoing the Deputy* #1402
‡‡*A Baby on the Ranch* #1410

Harlequin Special Edition

†††*A Match for the Doctor* #2117
†††*What the Single Dad Wants...* #2122
†*The Baby Wore a Badge* #2131
‡*Fortune's Valentine Bride* #2167
†††*Once Upon a Matchmaker* #2192
‡‡‡*Real Vintage Maverick* #2210

**Cavanaugh Justice*
***The Doctors Pulaski*
****Kate's Boys*
†*The Fortunes of Texas: Return to Red Rock*
††*The Baby Chase*
†††*Matchmaking Mamas*
‡*The Fortunes of Texas: Lost...and Found*
‡‡*Forever, Texas*
†*Montana Mavericks: The Texans Are Coming!*
‡*The Fortunes of Texas: Whirlwind Romance*
‡‡‡*Montana Mavericks: Back in the Saddle*

Silhouette Special Edition

****Diamond in the Rough* #1910
****The Bride with No Name* #1917
****Mistletoe and Miracles* #1941
†*Plain Jane and the Playboy* #1946
****Travis's Appeal* #1958

Other titles by this author available
in ebook format.

MARIE FERRARELLA

This *USA TODAY* bestselling and RITA® Award-winning author has written more than two hundred books for Harlequin Books, some under the name Marie Nicole. Her romances are beloved by fans worldwide. Visit her website, www.marieferrarella.com.

To
Sumay Li,
who is a joy
to know

Prologue

"Paula, I'm letting myself in with the key you gave me," Destiny Richardson called loudly as she stepped over the threshold into her younger sister's apartment. "It's Destiny, the sister you've been ignoring lately."

Again, she added silently.

She and Paula, her junior by a little more than three years, had finally gotten to a point in their relationship where they were getting along again. Where everything out of her mouth didn't get Paula's back up and mark the beginning of yet another prolonged argument that ended up with Paula not speaking to her for weeks at a time. That, mercifully, was now all behind them.

And then, for the past six weeks, it was as if Paula had stepped into a parallel universe. She was available only for a glimmer of time and then she'd disappear again. In between she'd return phone calls late and break lunch dates at the last minute.

Destiny had ridden it out for a couple of weeks, then finally asked her sister if this change in behavior was because of a man. Reluctantly—although she was glowing at the time—Paula had admitted that there *was* a new man in her life. But she wouldn't say any more, not even what his name was.

"Not yet, Des," she'd confided. "I don't want to jinx anything." Her eyes had all but danced as she'd added with a big grin, "He's just too good to be true."

Paula believed in the old adage that if something was too good to be true, it usually *was* too good to be true. But she'd bitten her tongue and said nothing, not wanting to jeopardize this new, improved relationship between her sister and her. It felt good to have Paula as a friend again, so she'd done her best to tread lightly and make no demands even though her gut had warned her that there was a problem.

She hated it when she was right in cases like this.

This morning, she'd gotten a text from Paula. It said simply: *He left me.* Thinking a few choice names directed at the man she'd never met, she'd called her sister almost immediately—and got no answer.

During the course of the day, she'd tried over and over again to reach Paula, using every single phone number associated with her sister. Home, work, cell, all with the same results. Paula wasn't picking up.

So, right after work, convinced that Paula was taking this breakup incredibly hard, she'd come to her sister's apartment and used the key Paula had given her for the very first time. She just wanted to make sure that her sister was all right.

She looked around now. Every single light in the up-scale, two-bedroom apartment was on.

"You better be home, kid," she called out, still addressing her words to the air. "Otherwise you're making the electric company very rich for no reason."

This was typical Paula, though. Her sister had a habit of turning on all the lights whenever she was depressed. She claimed it helped chase away the hopelessness she felt.

"Paula, where *are* you?" Destiny called, growing just a bit worried. Her mysterious "perfect" lover must have done a real number on her if Paula was too depressed even to answer her. "He's not worth it, you know," she said, making her way through the apartment. "Not worth being this upset over." She walked into Paula's bedroom. "If he could leave you just like that, you're better off without him. He doesn't sound very stable to me. He—"

For just half a second, Destiny froze in the doorway between the master bedroom and the lavishly remodeled bathroom.

Her heart stopped.

She'd found Paula.

"Oh, my God, Paula! Paula, what have you done?" she cried, racing into the bathroom.

The water in the bathtub had overflowed and spread out onto the tiled floor. The red tinge discolored everything. Her sister was immersed in the tub, and the water was red with her blood.

Paula's wrists were slashed.

Destiny Richardson had spent the past six years diligently working in the crime lab, at first part-time while she went to college and earned her degree in criminology, then, after graduation, full-time. From the very beginning, she had constantly gone the extra mile, putting in longer hours whenever she had a case.

In short order, she impressed Sean Cavanaugh, the man in charge of the crime lab's day shift. He promoted her to his chief assistant.

The first cardinal rule for a crime scene investigator was not to move or touch anything. But she wasn't a crime scene investigator tonight. She was Paula's sister, and she desperately wanted to save her.

But even as she grabbed her sister, ready to pull Paula out of the discolored water and perform CPR to try to save her, she knew it was too late. Paula's skin was abnormally cold and clammy.

And there was no heartbeat. Not even a faint flutter.

Paula was dead and had been for a number of hours.

"Oh, Paula, Paula, what did you do?" Destiny grieved, sinking down to the floor beside the bathtub. Water soaked into her clothing. She didn't care.

Because there was no one there and she had never felt so very alone in her life, Destiny allowed herself to break down for a moment.

Just for a moment.

She buried her face against the knees she'd brought up to her chest and sobbed as if her heart was breaking. Because it was.

Chapter 1

If police work wasn't for all intents and purposes the family business—doubly so now that he, along with the rest of his siblings and his father, had irrefutable proof that they comprised what amounted to the long-lost branch of the Cavanaugh family—Detective Logan Cavanaugh, known until recently as Logan Cavelli, would have been sorely tempted to give serious thought to another career choice.

Granted, Logan would have been the first to admit that he loved being a cop. Loved the idea that in some small way, he was fighting the good fight, righting wrongs and, along with his brothers and sisters, giving Aurora's everyday citizens that thin blue line that they knew was out there to protect them.

But there were times when the hours that went along with being a detective just about *killed* him. In the absolute sense, they were the same kind of hours that a doctor was expected to keep.

Doctors and police detectives were *always* expected to be on call—except that a doctor made a hell of a lot more money than he made, Logan thought darkly as he now drove—*alone*—to the address his lieutenant had handed to him when the man had torpedoed the very eventful evening he had planned for himself and his utterly luscious date.

One minute.

One lousy little minute. Sixty seconds and counting down, that's all he'd had left to his shift and then this evening with all its sensual promise would have become a reality.

He had already powered down his computer because Stacy, displaying a rare flair for punctuality, had just waltzed through the squad room door and had instantly made him the envy of every other breathing male in the vicinity.

Stacy, with the hips from heaven and the sinful mouth, who simply by walking across the floor could cause a eunuch to have lustful thoughts, was his date tonight. He was taking her out for dinner, dancing and a hot night of even hotter sex. The blond would-be model was his kind of woman. Gorgeous, passionate and totally uninterested in a permanent relationship.

Tonight had all the makings of an absolutely perfect evening.

But then his lieutenant had summoned him away from the doorway just as he was a hair's breadth away from being free and clear and making it into the hall.

No, that wasn't actually true, he thought in resignation, his hands tightening on the steering wheel until his knuckles were all but straining against his skin. Even if he had been in the middle of that passionate evening, enjoying all of Stacy's fabulously assembled attributes, his cell would have rung, calling him away from the ecstasy that shimmered before him, beckoning him onward because duty called.

When you're the next one up, you're the next one up. It was a simple, albeit hard, fact of life that went along with carrying a shield and a weapon.

So, instead of hot filet mignon, his dinner tonight would probably be the last couple of slices of the cold, leftover pizza in his refrigerator. And instead of a hot woman in his bed, he'd be sleeping alone tonight.

That was, if he got any sleep at all. A homicide detective with four years of experience under his belt, he'd learned that some cases unfurled slowly, inch by painful inch, while others ran you right into the ground from the moment you stepped into the crime scene arena and silently pledged to solve whatever needed solving.

Daylight had receded and the evening was making itself comfortable. He drove, looking for the right building, still wishing that he'd been engaged in a job that defined specific hours where the end of the day was the end of the day.

Wishing wouldn't make it so. Besides, Stacy, pouting prettily, had perked up at the promise of a rain check.

He laughed softly to himself, wondering if the woman thought that rain was actually involved in a rain check. He wouldn't put it past her. Luckily, it wasn't her brain that attracted him. After having to be on his toes all the time, it was nice to kick back sometimes and just let his brain rest.

Pulling up before the right apartment building, Logan saw that there were absolutely no empty spaces available along the long block. He debated driving to the parking structure on the next block, but he decided instead to double-park his vehicle in the fervent hope that his part in this wouldn't take all that long.

From the sketchy details he'd been given, it sounded pretty much like a cut-and-dried suicide—end of story. Once he verified that it was, maybe he could still even get hold of Stacy and at least get to enjoy the second half of the evening—that was, after all, the only thing that either one of them actually wanted from the other. Hot sex, enjoyable and a few minutes respite from the world they dealt with on a regular basis.

The thought made him smile as he got out of the car and locked it behind him.

The apartment in question was on the third floor. Once he got off the elevator, Logan found he didn't need to acquaint himself with the floor's layout or the way the apartment numbers were arranged to locate the one where his services were needed. The yellow tape and the stoic police officer standing guard did that for him.

Vaguely recognizing the weary-looking older officer, he nodded at the man. Their paths had probably crossed at one point or another, Logan thought.

"My dad here yet?"

It was actually meant as a rhetorical question. This was the tail end of the day shift, but his father, the head of the CSI day lab, was dedicated beyond belief. He was the one who had instilled his work ethic in him and his siblings long before they had discovered that they were related to the Cavanaughs.

Besides, there was all this yellow tape across the front of the entrance, a sure sign that his father and some of the team who worked for him were in there, carefully documenting and preserving everything with such precision it would have absolutely stunned the average mind.

The officer, Dale Hanlon, shook his head. "No, not yet."

Logan stopped, surprised as he turned to regard the officer. Unless there were multiple crime scenes happening at once—something that had yet to occur in Aurora—in the past year—his father had taken to being present with his team at each crime scene that they processed.

This wasn't making any sense to him. "Then who put up all this yellow tape?" he asked.

"I did."

The low, controlled female voice came from behind him. The vague thought that the voice was more suited to an intimate dinner than a crime scene crossed Logan's mind as he turned around again.

Logan found himself looking into the saddest blue eyes he'd ever seen.

They were also, quite possibly, the bluest eyes he'd ever seen, which was saying a great deal considering that the Cavanaughs were fairly littered with members who had blue eyes of all hues and shades.

The eyes were set in a striking, heart-shaped face that would have easily launched a thousand love songs, he couldn't help thinking. Sometimes, Logan decided, this job did have its perks.

"Are you part of the crime scene investigation unit?" Logan heard himself asking as he quickly assessed the slender, pale-looking blonde standing before him. "Or do you just have a thing for crime scene tape?" he quipped wryly, trying to lighten the moment. She seemed much too serious for someone so young. He knew this job, especially this part of the job, could really get to people if they didn't take any precautions and insulate themselves properly.

His flippant manner caught Destiny off guard for a second. Since the officer at the door hadn't tried to turn the man away, that had to mean that he was with the Aurora police force.

Terrific. Just her luck. They'd sent a brash, cocky detective who looked as if he was in love with the sound of his own voice and, most likely, with the image he saw in his bathroom mirror each morning. Dark-haired, green-eyed, he was as handsome as they came, and she was certain that he knew it.

She was familiar with the type, and right now it was the last thing she needed. She needed a professional detective, not a male model.

"I'm with the crime scene investigation unit," she told him, her voice low and remarkably stoic. She surprised herself.

It was all she could do to hold it together. Part of Destiny still didn't believe that any of this was actually happening. The other part felt as if she was slowly slipping into shock and would, at any moment, just completely lose it.

You can't. If you do, you won't be able to help Paula.

The moment the thought formed, it struck Destiny as ironic. After all, at this point *nothing* would help Paula. Nothing was going to bring her back.

Destiny struggled to keep her angry tears in check.

Logan nodded, taking the attractive woman's information at face value. "I guess this is just an open-and-shut case," he surmised. "A suicide," he added, telling her what the lieutenant had told him. Then, his mouth curving in a particularly captivating smile, he asked, "How is it that I've never seen you before?" He would have certainly remembered someone who looked like her. He had a feeling that if she smiled, she could light up a room. Even somber, there was something exceedingly attractive and compelling about her. "Are you new to the team?"

She didn't bother answering his last question. At another time and place, she might have been more than mildly interested in his attention. Destiny wasn't averse to having an occasional good time, as long as no promises were exchanged or expected. She was married to her work, and most of the men she'd encountered felt that they should come first in a woman's life, not second.

Right now, all her energy was focused on not breaking down and, more important than that, on finding who had done this to her sister.

"It's not a suicide," Destiny informed the detective firmly.

About to walk to where he could view the deceased's body, Logan turned instead and focused on the intense crime scene investigator. She sounded as if there was no room for argument.

"Why?" he asked, the detective in him pushing the playboy far into the background. "Did you find something that would indicate that the woman was murdered?"

"Not yet," Destiny answered between clenched teeth. "But I will."

Okay, he was officially confused, Logan thought. Was there some sort of an agenda he was missing? Exactly what did this woman mean by "not yet"? What did she know that he didn't? He didn't like playing catch-up.

"If there are no indications that it's *not* a suicide, what makes you think that it isn't?" he asked the shapely blonde.

"Because she *wouldn't* commit suicide," Destiny informed him heatedly.

Really curious now, Logan looked at the young woman who, he realized, had more going on, even without the aid of painted-on clothing, than Stacy ever did. She didn't reek of raw sex, but there was a subtle promise there that intrigued him. A lot.

Since the department paid him to solve cases, not ruminate on beautiful women who said baseless things, Logan forced himself to focus on the wild claim the crime scene investigator had just made and not the fact that the words had come out of nearly perfect lips.

"And you know this because...?"

A very tempting chin shot up like a silent challenge. "Because she's my sister."

It took him a second to absorb that. "You weren't called in, were you?" Logan guessed.

No, she hadn't been. She'd come here looking for answers and had wound up face-to-face with a dreadful question: Who killed Paula?

"I did the calling," she told him.

As if in a bad dream, once she knew that Paula was beyond resuscitating and she'd stopped crying, she'd pulled herself together and called her boss, even though protocol would have had her calling 911 first.

The sound of Sean Cavanaugh's voice had almost made her lose it again, but Destiny had managed to hold herself together enough to describe what she'd found when she'd walked into her sister's apartment. Sean in turn had set everything else in motion, promising to be there as soon as he possibly could. He told her not to leave.

As if she could.

With no knowledge of what had taken place between his father and the crime scene investigator, Logan had a different take on things.

"You can't be here," he told her, transforming from a devil-may-care man who enjoyed his share of the night-life to a homicide detective who was considered to be damn good at his job.

Logan saw the woman's slender shoulders stiffen as if she'd been jabbed with a hot poker. She reminded him of a soldier, galvanized in order to withstand what-ever came her way.

The flash of anger in her eyes was almost mesmer-izing to him.

"The hell I can't," she snapped. "She's my baby sis-ter and the only family I have left. Had left," Destiny amended, trying hard not to allow the words to choke off her air supply. "Somebody killed her, and I intend to find out who."

Having brothers and sisters of his own, Logan could easily relate to the way she felt. But she still needed to go. "I get it, but leave it up to—"

"To who?" Destiny demanded. "To you? To the pro-fessionals?" She guessed at the word he was about to use. "I *am* one of the professionals."

That might be true, but there was another, bigger factor that she was apparently missing—or deliberately ignoring. "You're also personally involved—"

"You *bet* I am," Destiny snapped, her eyes flashing again, "and no rules and regulations are going to make me stand on the sidelines like some clueless civilian, waiting for someone to find something that would point to my sister's killer—especially when they're not even going to be looking."

"Now wait a minute—"

No, she wasn't going to "wait a minute." And she certainly wasn't going to allow him to snow her with rhetoric.

"A minute ago, you were all ready to write this off as a suicide. You were willing to go with what you saw— or *thought* you saw."

Only up to a point. Where did she get off, criticizing his work if she hadn't seen him in action? Gorgeous or not, she needed to be told a few things and put in her place.

"Not if the autopsy contradicts the idea of a suicide."

Autopsy.

The very word brought up a chilling scenario with it. Someone cutting up her little sister, reducing Paula to a mass of body organs examined, weighed, catalogued and then impersonally stuffed back into her body like wrinkled tissue paper that has served its purpose.

Suddenly, Destiny could hardly bear the wave of pain she felt.

Logan saw the horror that washed over the woman's fine-boned features before she apparently got herself under control again. Observing her, he had to admit he felt really sorry for the woman. He knew how he would have reacted if that was Bridget, or Kendra, or Kari in the next room.

No rules or orders would have kept him on the sidelines. If he couldn't have been part of the investigation outright, he would have found a way to conduct his own investigation covertly until he found answers that satisfied him.

Until he found the killer.

He felt a budding respect as he looked at the woman for the first time, not assessing her comely features but taking measure of the person who existed beneath. Thinking of what she was feeling and taking stock of what had to be crossing her mind right now.

Logan relented, backing off from his initial stand.

"Look, what if I promise to keep you filled in? Will that be enough for you?"

The moment the words emerged from his mouth, he knew they had come out wrong. He made it sound as if he was trying to dismiss her. He wasn't doing anything of the kind.

Destiny tossed her head, anger and sadness mingling with the very stubborn streak that had seen her through a less than typical childhood, one that would have conquered a lesser person. And she had been a child at the time.

"No, sorry, not good enough," she fired back.

"He's right, you know."

She didn't have to turn around and look to know who was behind her. But she turned around anyway. Turned around and looked up at the man she respected and secretly regarded as the father she hadn't had for all these many years, not since he'd walked out on her, Paula and their mother.

"I thought you'd be on my side," she said to Sean. She was more than a little disappointed to hear him taking the side of company policy.

"I am *always* on your side," Sean reminded her kindly. "But the rules are clear about working on a case that you're personally involved in."

She knew all the rules backward and forward. She also knew they weren't going to stop her from working this investigation.

"Sean, please," she implored hoarsely, her voice brimming with emotion. She laid a hand on Sean's arm in mute supplication.

"Of course," Sean continued loftily, as if she hadn't said anything, "you are a grown woman and I can't be expected to tie you up and throw you into some corner if you happen to do some poking around into the present case behind my back." He saw his son staring at him, undoubtedly surprised at this break with protocol. "Oh, like you and those brothers and sisters of yours never bent a single rule," he mocked.

"Not saying we didn't," Logan replied to his father, deliberately flying above this minefield. "But I've got to say that I'm really surprised that you're considering it."

"Not considering it," Sean corrected, putting down his fully loaded case that he meticulously organized at least once a week. "But well, what happens when I'm not looking, happens," he told his son innocently. "Now, if you'll excuse me, I believe the actual scene of the crime is in through there?" He pointed to the bedroom, looking to Destiny for confirmation.

Destiny only half nodded. "That's the way to the bathroom," she confirmed. "Whether or not that's the actual scene of the crime remains to be seen."

Sean gave her an encouraging smile. "An open mind is the best way to approach anything," he agreed.

With that, he walked ahead of his son and the young woman to process this particular crime scene.

Chapter 2

Following Sean Cavanaugh through the bedroom and into the bathroom where her sister's body was, Destiny could feel every single bone in her own body stiffening as the battle began all over again. Her protective instincts warred with the ones she had developed as a crime scene investigator.

The latter dictated adherence to the first cardinal rule of investigation: that nothing was to be touched, nothing was to be moved. It was of the utmost importance that the scene be preserved just as it was when the deceased died. This had to be done to piece together facts leading up to that person's final moments. And, with that, the identity of the killer, if there was one.

But Destiny's protective instincts were just as deeply rooted within her, if not more so. She was the older sister, the one who had always looked out for Paula.

Yeah, and how's that going for you? Destiny silently mocked herself.

Being the older sister hadn't been easy. Though she had never doubted her sister's love for her, Paula had fought her all the way, desperately wanting to assert her independence.

"I'm a big girl now, Destiny. You can't hover over me forever."

Destiny could feel the corners of her eyes beginning to sting again as she struggled for the umpteenth time to hold back her tears.

Yeah, well, you would have done better if I had hovered, Destiny couldn't help thinking now. There was no doubt in her mind that Paula would be alive right now if she *had* hovered.

If.

Her protective instincts had made her want to cover Paula up, to give her sister some small semblance of modesty and dignity by draping something over her— at least a towel. She didn't want to leave her where everyone coming into the beige-and-blue-tiled bathroom could see her like this, utterly naked and exposed.

As if sensing her turmoil, Sean told her, "I promise I'll make this as quick as I can, Destiny."

She was grateful to him for his kindness. Pressing her lips together, Destiny nodded, doing her best to smile her thanks and succeeding only marginally.

"Thank you," she said hoarsely.

Logan, who had entered behind his father and the victim's sister, squatted down now, his attention focused on the opened cell phone that apparently had slipped from the dead woman's hand just as life had ebbed away from her.

The cell phone was in the open position and it was still turned on. As he crouched closer to it, Logan could see that there was a text message on the screen. One last message just before death had found her.

Was it a last-minute regret and a plea for help? Or was this intended to be a virtual version of a suicide note?

Using his handkerchief to keep from getting his fingerprints on the phone or contaminating any prints besides the victim's on the device, Logan was about to pick it up when he stopped and looked over toward his father. "Did you already take a picture of this?"

"Tagged and photographed," Sean answered as he continued examining Destiny's sister.

Logan lifted the phone and looked at the screen. There were only three words in the text message: *He left me.*

"We need to find out who this number belongs to," Logan said, thinking out loud as he examined the cell number the message had been sent to.

"Not necessary," Destiny told him stoically.

Each word she uttered felt as if it scraped along an incredibly dry tongue. Her whole mouth felt like a desert in the midst of a seven-year drought. And she was having trouble getting air into her lungs. Part of her was numb, the other was almost on fire.

"She texted you?" Logan guessed, glancing toward her and reading her body language.

Right now, the woman appeared to be shut down

tighter than Fort Knox. Logan absently wondered what it would take to loosen her up, then dismissed the thought since right now, knowing that wasn't going to help him. Thinking of her as a woman was completely out of line. She was the victim's sister and his father's assistant, nothing else.

At least, not right now.

Logan caught himself hoping that there would be a later.

Destiny heard the detective's voice as if it had originated in an echo chamber. It sounded as if it was coming at her from a great distance.

She blinked, forcing herself to stay focused. If she let her mind wander, she wouldn't make it out of this room without coming apart. She'd already cried once. That was all she could afford to grieve. She had work to do.

"Yes, it's my number. I called her back almost immediately after she sent the message, but she didn't pick up." She pressed her lips together, taking a breath before continuing. Her voice sounded strained. "I'd been calling her all day without a response, so I got worried."

"Why?" Logan asked. "Was she unstable? Were you afraid that she was likely to harm herself?"

Destiny stared at him. What was he talking about? He didn't know Paula. He had no right to his assumptions. She took offense at the implication behind his questions.

"I got worried because I'm her *sister,*" she retorted angrily. "Because Paula normally keeps in touch. And she doesn't send short text messages." The three-word text was out of character for Paula. "She goes on and on, whether it's a phone call, a text or in person. My sister is—was," she corrected herself painfully, "not a person of a few words. She never said anything in three words that she could say in forty."

He thought of pointing out that distraught people, especially people about to commit suicide, didn't always conform to their normal behavior, but he had a feeling she wasn't in the mood to be contradicted.

Instead, he focused on another piece of the puzzle. "Who's this 'him' she's referring to?" he asked.

"I don't know."

Destiny took a deep breath, angry with herself for not having pushed when Paula had opted to keep the man's name a secret. If she'd badgered Paula enough, she *knew* Paula would have finally caved in. Why hadn't she pushed? Why had she just elected to respect her sister's boundaries? At the very least, this mystery man of Paula's could give them insight to her frame of mind the last time he saw her as he left.

If he'd left her, Destiny amended, ruling out nothing.

"You don't know?" Logan echoed, more than mildly surprised. "Then you two weren't close?" That was the only conclusion he could draw.

"No, we were," Destiny insisted. "Very close." They had been that way once and they had gotten that way again just in the past couple of years.

"Then why don't you know the name of the guy your sister was seeing?"

Because I'm an idiot.

"Paula was a little superstitious. She said she didn't

want to jinx the relationship by saying anything about it too soon."

God, that sounded so lame, so childish now that she said it out loud, Destiny thought, on the edge of exasperated despair. Why hadn't she pushed? Insisted? Maybe if she'd known more of the details, she could have somehow prevented this. Even though she didn't believe in her heart of hearts that her sister had done this, had committed suicide, a tiny part of her was afraid she had.

"All she'd tell me was that he was someone 'important.' And, that for now, he wanted to keep their relationship 'special' by keeping it out of the public eye. Apparently, I was part of the public eye," Destiny said with barely controlled frustration.

Most likely, the guy was married, Logan thought, and when he'd decided to go back to his wife, the victim had killed herself.

"And you don't think that this is a suicide?" Logan asked again. It was obvious from his tone that he felt that the evidence they'd reviewed so far clearly pointed in that direction.

"No," Destiny said with feeling. "If this 'important' bastard had left her, she wouldn't have killed herself. Paula was the type to have gone upside his head, to have raised a stink, not taken the breakup docilely, given up all hope and killed herself." She raised her chin defiantly as she added, "I know my sister. That's just not like her."

Did anyone really know anyone else? Logan wondered. Of late, since the big revelation that had jolted his family down to their roots, he'd faced that question more than once.

"That's what you *think*," Logan pointed out. And, as far as he was concerned, there was an entire world of difference between prejudiced perception and actual fact.

"No," Destiny said flatly. "That's what I *know*. My sister believed in revenge," she was quick to add, seeing the suspicious light coming into the detective's all-but-magnetic green eyes. "And by that, I mean she would have dolled herself up, found the first good-looking male she could and deliberately shown up somewhere where she knew that 'Mr. Special' would most likely be. Then she would have flaunted the fact that she was having an exceptionally good time with someone new and gorgeous. Paula was not the kind to just give up," she insisted. "She was stubborn that way."

How long was it going to take to get used to referring to Paula in the past tense? Destiny wondered, her heart aching in her chest.

"I take it stubbornness runs in the family?" Logan surmised, watching her. There was just a hint of an appreciative smile on his lips.

Her blue eyes narrowed into slits. "Damn straight it does."

"You might be right," Sean interjected as if there was no other conversation taking place. Having completed his preliminary examination of the dead woman, he straightened up.

"About which part?" Logan asked, just taking it for

granted that his father was talking to him and not to the sexy, headstrong woman before him.

Instead of answering his son immediately, Sean focused his attention on the person in the room who needed him the most.

"Was your sister right-handed?" he asked Destiny.

She shook her head. "No, Paula was left-handed. Why?" Had he found something to substantiate her gut feeling that her sister hadn't taken her own life? Without realizing it, Destiny began to pray.

"Just trying to get my facts straight," Sean said thoughtfully, never one to give away anything too soon. Pausing a moment longer, he then said, "I don't believe she killed herself."

Yes!

The relief that flooded through her limbs just about took Destiny's breath away. At least she wasn't going to have to fight everyone tooth and nail about this. If the head of the crime lab backed her up, the battle over that at least was over. Now the major one began: finding Paula's killer.

"Thank you," she said to Sean. The words came out on a nearly breathless sigh.

While he knew that his father wouldn't just say something like that to put his assistant at ease, Logan still wanted proof.

"What makes you say that?" he asked his father.

"When a person slashes their wrists, depending on whether they're right-handed or left-handed, the cut is deeper on the opposite wrist since they're using their good hand."

If the person followed regular procedure, Logan thought. Maybe this one hadn't. "She might have slashed her right wrist first," Logan suggested. "That would have made her right hand weaker when she was delivering the final cut."

"True," Sean allowed.

Concerned, Destiny immediately asked, "Then you're changing your mind?"

Again, rather than answering directly, Sean turned toward his son, opting for a demonstration. "If you were to slash your wrists, how would you go about it?" he asked.

Logan firmly believed that there wasn't anything in the world that would cause him to give up all hope and just apathetically end his life.

"I wouldn't," Logan said flatly.

"Good to know," his father murmured. "But if you did, if you put yourself in the place of someone who'd lost all hope and given up wanting to live," Sean proposed, "*how* would you slash your wrists?"

Logan honestly didn't know what his father was getting at. "The usual way," he answered with a careless shrug.

"Show me," Sean urged. Taking a pen out of his breast pocket, he handed it to Logan. "Pretend this is a knife. Show me how you'd go about 'slashing' your wrists if you were committing suicide."

With another, somewhat more pronounced shrug, Logan took the pen from his father and then, holding it in his right hand, traced a slightly slanted line from left to right across his left wrist. And then, changing hands, he took the pen into his left hand and reversed the process, "slashing" his right wrist from right to left with the imaginary knife. Both times the lines he created were slightly slanted, going from higher to lower.

"Okay, consider them slashed," Logan said, handing the pen back to his father. His curiosity had been piqued. "Now what?"

"Now you'd bleed out," Sean said matter-of-factly. "All right, keeping your methodical procedure in mind, I want you to take a look at Paula's wrists," he told both his son and his assistant. "What do you see?"

Each wrist had a long, deep cut going across it. "Slashes," Logan answered.

Destiny narrowed her eyes, distancing herself from the actual person in the bathtub and focusing only on the victim's wrists. She looked intently at the cuts that had caused her sister to die.

After scrutinizing the two cuts, she felt no more enlightened than she had been at the outset.

Shaking her head, she said, "I don't—"

"Look carefully," Sean repeated, cutting her off.

"I did," she protested.

And then she saw it, saw what Sean was trying to point out without actually physically doing it. Her eyes widened and she looked at him.

"The slashes are both going in the same direction!" But there was more than just that, she realized. "And they're both upside down."

Instead of slanting slightly at the top and then dipping down as it reached the opposite side, each cut seemed to go from the bottom to the top, left to right, on both wrists.

"This is too awkward," Destiny concluded, her excitement growing. And then she repeated what she had been maintaining all along. "Paula couldn't have done this to herself. Someone else had to have done it to her."

He could see his father trying to spare his assistant and make her feel better, but there were other matters to consider, Logan thought.

"There's no sign of a struggle," he pointed out, then continued, "There's no huge amount of water along the perimeter of the old-fashioned tub, leaving the actual tub low, as if there'd been a wild, last-minute struggle. There are no outstanding bruises visible on the victim's body, and her long, salon-applied nails all seem to be intact. They wouldn't have been if she was fighting for her life."

"There wouldn't be any struggle if the victim was drugged," Sean told his son, his voice as mild as if he were discussing the garden section of the Sunday paper. Turning, Sean pointed to the wine goblet he had already photographed and that now stood, bagged, on the bathroom floor exactly where he had found it. "A simple analysis can tell us about that."

Logan still didn't see that as proof. "A lot of suicides build up their courage with a drink first. Maybe the victim wanted to make sure that she wouldn't experience a last-minute surge of regret that might cause her to stop what she was doing." He looked at his father. "Despondence can do that to you."

"Maybe to you," Destiny fired back. "But not to

Paula. She did *not* kill herself. I'd stake my badge on it," she insisted.

"Besides," Sean interjected, "there are the cuts to her wrists. Our killer obviously slipped up there." Returning the items he'd taken out previously, as well as packing up the samples he'd taken into his case, Sean glanced at Destiny. "Are you absolutely sure your sister never mentioned this man's name? Dropped a hint, used initials? Something like that?"

To each suggestion, Destiny could only shake her head no. Each time she did so, she felt her frustration growing larger and larger.

"No."

The truth of it was that despite her initial concerns, she'd been really hopeful that Paula was finally looking to settle into a lasting relationship. And due to that, she hadn't wanted to cause any waves by hounding her sister for details.

"And you didn't press her?" Logan asked incredulously. What kind of a woman didn't ask for details? he couldn't help wondering. Was it because she was too wrapped up in her own love life? Was there some guy she was going to go running home to, to cry on his shoulder?

From out of nowhere, Logan felt just the slightest prick of jealousy. He shrugged it off, thinking he was just frustrated because he'd had to break his date with Stacy.

Destiny could only shrug impotently. "I figured she'd tell me when she was ready."

He couldn't help staring at her. Was she for real? If

this had been one of his sisters, the other two would have been all over her until she finally broke. The life expectancy of a secret in the household where he'd grown up had been about a day and a half—if the one with the secret was in a coma.

"Wow, a woman with no curiosity," he marveled, only half in jest. "I thought that was like, you know, an urban myth or something. Kind of like a unicorn," he tagged on.

If nothing else, the man was mixing his metaphors. He was also being colossally annoying.

"Unicorns don't wander around urban areas," she pointed out, irritated at the detective's flippant manner and not bothering to hide the fact, even if he was Sean's son. Maybe he was adopted, she thought. Her eyes narrowed as she pinned him with a glare. "Are you going to take this seriously or not?" she asked.

"I'm officially ruling this a murder," Sean announced, interrupting what appeared to be an argument in the making—he knew for a fact that Logan didn't like being challenged. "Don't worry. He'll take it seriously now," he assured his assistant with a note of finality in his voice.

She was overreacting. Her sister's murder—just finding Paula this way—was making her lose her perspective. If she continued down this road, then she really would wind up being thrown off the case.

And soon.

At the very least, she wasn't any good to anyone if she unraveled this way.

Destiny took in a deep, shaky breath, getting herself back under control. Her spine snapped into place, ramrod straight.

"Sorry," she said to Sean.

"You have nothing to be sorry about," Sean told her warmly. Placing a fatherly arm around her shoulders, he gently escorted Destiny from the room.

The sound of fresh activity was heard coming from the living room. The M.E.'s team had just arrived, pushing a gurney between them.

Nodding at the duo, Sean said, "The victim's in the bathtub. She's had a preliminary workup and is ready to go."

"It's a suicide, right?" one of the men asked, looking at the sheet attached to his clipboard. The latter was lying on top of the gurney.

"No, it's a homicide," Logan corrected, answering for his father.

He wasn't oblivious to the relieved smile that Destiny shot him. Though it lasted only half a second, he'd been right. Her smile did have the makings to light up a room.

Hearing what Logan said, one of the two men sighed and shook his head. "It's going to be another long night," he anticipated, addressing his words to no one in particular.

"C'mon, don't just stand there and make it any longer," the other man prodded.

Pushing the gurney before them, they entered the next room.

Once they were gone, Sean turned to Destiny. "I should be the one who's saying he's sorry," he said to her, continuing what he was saying before the two assistants from the M.E.'s office had entered the apartment. "And I am. I am *deeply* sorry for your loss," he emphasized. "And we *will* find the person responsible for this, Destiny," he said. "I give you my word."

Destiny blinked back her tears. It felt as if she'd been fighting them all along. Her supervisor wasn't making things any easier for her.

"I believe you," she murmured, her voice hardly above a whisper. Any louder and she knew she would risk breaking down entirely.

Again.

To the best of Logan's knowledge, it was the first time he'd ever heard his father make a promise that he wasn't a hundred percent certain ahead of time that he could back up.

This assistant had to mean a lot to him, he concluded, then couldn't help wondering why.

Chapter 3

"Were you two on the outs?" Logan asked Destiny as his father continued processing the rest of the small apartment.

Why did he keep coming back to that?

"No. She was my only family. We were close—as close as two people who lived two different, busy lives could be," she qualified, emphasizing the word *busy*. "We didn't get together as much as I would have liked, but that couldn't have been helped." Her eyes narrowed slightly as she regarded Logan, looking for some kind of an indication as to what was really on his mind. She began to suspect that he wasn't the typical vapid, shallow pretty boy. There was substance, a trait she'd always found far sexier than looks.

But right now, she was in a place where things like that didn't matter.

"Why are you asking?" she asked.

He answered her question with a question. "Is there any reason you can think of why she wouldn't have told you who she was seeing?"

Logan was still having a lot of trouble swallowing the scenario the woman's sister had given him. All three of his sisters not only knew everything there was to know about each other's boyfriends, or, in Bridget's case, her fiancé, they were also aware of their friends' current dates. He couldn't fathom a woman who was willingly oblivious to that sort of information—and actually content to remain that way.

Suppressing a sigh, she said, "Probably to avoid hearing me tell her to go slow and to be careful." She saw the question in the detective's eyes. Under another set of circumstances, they might have even been intriguing eyes. Right now, they were just annoyingly probing. "My sister doesn't—didn't," she corrected herself, hating the fact that she had to, "have the greatest track record when it came to picking men. They were all very good-looking on the outside. On the inside, not so much."

Holding her hand out, she waffled it to indicate just how much each of the previous men in her sister's life had deviated from the straight-and-narrow path. There hadn't been a decent one in the lot.

"So in other words, she didn't give you any details about who she was seeing because she didn't want you to be judgmental," Logan concluded succinctly.

She nodded, wishing with all her heart that she hadn't come down as hard on Paula over the last one as she had. Not that he didn't deserve every insulting adjective she had hurled at his memory. Slick, charming, with a Southern drawl, Bo Wilkins had managed to deplete half of Paula's bank account—granted, that didn't exactly amount to a king's ransom, but it was *still* Paula's money—before just vanishing off the face of the earth.

She'd begged Paula to let her know the next time she gave away her heart, because she'd said she intended to run a check on whomever the next Romeo was. If no prior arrests came up, then at least her sister would have a fighting chance of keeping the fillings in her teeth.

Paula hadn't found that funny, she recalled. And she deliberately hadn't said anything about meeting someone new—until she'd been pinned down.

That was when Paula had told her that she didn't want to say anything yet because she didn't want to jinx the relationship. And, if it became serious, *then* she would say something.

Given that, Destiny had seen no reason to push.

But apparently, it *had* been serious. Which meant that Paula had lied to her, Destiny realized with a sharp pang. It obviously had to have been serious if Paula had been despondent enough to text that message to her.

If she texted that message, a little voice in Destiny's head whispered.

Her eyes widened as the thought sank in.

What if Paula hadn't even been the one to text that message? What if her killer had? The same killer who had botched the appearance of a suicide by slashing her wrists upside down.

Trying not to get ahead of herself, she turned toward Sean. "We have to process her cell phone for any fingerprints on the keypad that aren't hers. The guy probably wore gloves, but maybe he got careless...."

Destiny's voice trailed off as she made eye contact with her supervisor. He wasn't saying anything, just letting her talk, but she could see by the expression on his face that he was already way ahead of her. He always seemed to be two steps ahead of everyone.

"You already thought of that," she said, nodding her head.

"We're on the same page," Sean told her kindly. "Same page that Logan's on," he said, nodding toward his son.

Feeling anxious and yet dull-witted at the same time, an area she had never inhabited before, Destiny turned toward the detective, curious why he wasn't saying anything.

The answer to that was simple. Because he wasn't standing there anymore.

"Cavanaugh?" she called, raising her voice.

"In here," Logan answered, his voice floating back to her from the back of the apartment.

Apparently a thought had occurred to him and he'd gone back into the bedroom to look at something, or *for* something.

Actually, the man had gone back to the bathroom, Destiny realized as she followed the sound of the detective's deep voice.

As she entered the bedroom, she had to shift to one side. The medical examiner's team had slipped Paula's body into that one-size-fits-all black body bag and was now wheeling her sister back out. Once outside the building, they'd put her into the coroner's van they'd driven over here.

Paula didn't like the color black, Destiny recalled with a pang. It was the only color missing from her meticulously arranged wardrobe.

"Black is the color of death, Destiny. I don't want it anywhere near me."

It is now, pumpkin. It is now, Destiny thought, feeling her heart twist inside of her.

Walking into the bathroom, painfully aware that her sister was no longer here—no longer anywhere—she found Logan standing before the medicine cabinet. The door was open and the detective was peering at the shelves. He was obviously taking inventory of what was inside. She didn't exactly care for the thoughtful frown she saw on his face.

Now what?

Bracing herself, thinking that she would have to defend her sister again, Destiny forced herself to ask, "What?"

Logan read the generic name imprinted on the container's label again. This put a crimp in the woman's theory. He held the container up so that she could see it, as well.

"This was just filled," he told her.

She had no idea what "this" was but had a feeling she wouldn't be happy once she heard the answer.

Even so, though she knew Logan had to do it, she resented this man's prying into her sister's life. And, by proxy, into her life. Resented the lack of understanding and compassion in his voice.

Granted, as a good detective, he was supposed to be impartial, but keeping this kind of a distance between himself and the victim didn't help him understand the kind of person her sister had been. Didn't make him fiercely want to solve this tragic crime because the world was that much the lesser for the loss of her.

Taking yet another breath, Destiny was satisfied that her voice wouldn't crack. Only then did she finally answer him. "Yes, so?"

Still holding the bottle up, he shook it. Hard. There was no sound to correspond with the movement, no pills being disturbed and forced to rattle around the small container.

"So it's empty," he pointed out needlessly. "According to the date it was filled, there should be approximately twenty-five pills in here. There aren't." He looked at her. "What do you want to bet that toxicology is going to find that those pills are in your sister's system? Her wrists didn't need to be slashed," he told her. "Your sister swallowed enough of these things to have killed a small horse."

"Or was forced to swallow," Destiny interjected. She wasn't going to let him just forget about what his father had pointed out. Evidence that pointed to her sister being murdered.

"There's no sign of a struggle, remember? Maybe, before the full effects of the pills kicked in, your sister actually *did* try to slash her wrists but she was so loopy from the pills that she did an awkward, botched job of it."

Taking the vial from him, Destiny turned the container around so she could read the label. When she did, the name of the drug was vaguely familiar. Her sister was taking prescription sleeping pills, one of the newer ones on the market.

"Ever since we were little, my sister has had trouble sleeping. When these came on the market—" she nodded at the empty container "—and she tried them, she was overjoyed. She'd finally found something that worked. But she never took more than the prescribed dosage," Destiny maintained firmly. "It wasn't because she was a saint," she added angrily, reading the skepticism in Logan's eyes. "She just didn't want to feel drugged in the morning. The idea of falling asleep behind the wheel while driving to work terrified her," she emphasized.

Logan took back the container, intending on giving it to his father to send to toxicology.

"Still, over time, people develop a tolerance for medications. Maybe she found that one pill wasn't enough for her anymore and she took two—and then more. Or maybe she just wanted to sleep forever because her boyfriend dumped her."

He was back to that again. What was he, Johnny One-note? she thought angrily. How many ways did she have to say this before it finally sank into the thick skull of his?

"No," Destiny insisted with feeling. "Paula wouldn't have done that. Someone killed my sister," she said, enunciating each word separately. "I don't know who it was, but I do know that Paula didn't do it herself—accidentally or otherwise," Destiny added in case he was going to suggest that next.

"All right," Logan relented.

His father's lead assistant wasn't about to come around to his side or even remotely entertain the idea that her sister had committed suicide. And since his father seemed to believe that someone else had delivered the slash marks to the young woman's wrists, for the time being he'd go along with the popular theory.

Besides, he really didn't enjoy upsetting her, considering that she was still dealing with the shock of finding her sister dead.

"We'll approach it that way for now." Leaving the bathroom, still holding the prescription container with his handkerchief wrapped around it, Logan handed it to his father.

"The pills are probably all in her stomach," he told him not as his father, but as the head of the crime scene lab.

"You're most likely right," Sean agreed. "Whoever killed her probably slipped the pills into her drink. That way there'd be no resistance to what he was going to do next." He lowered his voice so that only Logan could hear. "Poor thing never stood a chance."

Logan nodded vaguely. He wasn't doing anyone any good just standing here, he decided, and announced, "I'm going to canvass the floor, see if anyone heard or saw anything out of the ordinary."

"But you don't think so," Destiny surmised.

"I didn't say that," Logan maintained. He didn't like being second-guessed. For the most part, he liked to think that on the job he was unreadable. He prided himself on that.

Besides, he was always open to possibilities. This job consisted of equal parts skill *and* luck.

"Hey, you never know. Stranger things have happened. And not everyone works nine to five," he added cavalierly. "So maybe someone *did* hear something." Logan paused just next to his father as he began to head out the front door. "Maybe I'll see you this Sunday." It was as close as he allowed himself to get to making a commitment that involved his new family.

"Maybe," Sean echoed with a faint nod.

"Sunday?" Destiny repeated, her smattering of curiosity getting the better of her when it came to this handsome, arrogant would-be crime fighter. "What's this Sunday?"

Since he knew that this woman worked closely with his father—it had to be closely for his father to display this kind of regard for her, treating her as if she was another one of his daughters—he was surprised that she didn't know.

"The former chief of police, my new uncle," he added, amused by the whole concept of getting such a huge number of brand-new blood relatives at his age. "He likes to throw family get-togethers. Word has it that any of us can drop by his table to get a full breakfast any day of the week, but apparently he goes all out on Sundays.

"My father is settling into this new life and doing

his best to show up every Sunday to prove how serious
he is about being assimilated by the Cavanaughs—and
making up for lost time."

Destiny nodded. Though Sean Cavanaugh wasn't an
overly talkative man, he had shared some of this with
her already. She had to admit that she rather liked the
fact that he confided to her about this new venue of his
private life.

It also made her realize how much she missed having a family of her own, people to talk to and use as
sounding boards. People who cared how she felt and if
she was getting enough sleep or running herself into
the ground. After her mother had died, there'd been
only Paula. And now even she was gone. That left only
her, and it was true what they said. One *is* the loneli-
est number.

"Must be nice having more family than you know
what to do with," she commented, trying to sound off-
handed.

He would have had to have been completely deaf
to have missed the wistfulness in her voice. Although
he wasn't given to being touchy-feely and was rather
careless at times about other people's feelings, Logan
upbraided himself now for not realizing that he was
talking about family life to a woman who no longer
had one.

He felt a genuine stab of guilt.

The next moment he heard himself trying to make
amends. "Feel free to drop by on any morning or on
Sunday," he added. "The man goes all out then," he repeated. When he saw her looking at him, obviously puz-

zled, he guessed at what was going through her mind. "Don't worry, the chief won't mind."

"But you just said that he had family gatherings," she pointed out. And right now, she was part of no one's family.

"To the chief, anyone who's part of the force is family."

Okay, so maybe the handsome detective wasn't just an empty vessel. He was being kind to her because she was alone. She got that. But she was no one's charity case. Allowing a spasmodic smile to reach her lips, then go, she thanked him.

"I'll keep that in mind."

Logan knew a brush-off when he heard one, and ordinarily he'd just let it ride. But this woman was obviously someone special to his father, and initially he had been rather coarsely oblivious with her.

"No, really," he emphasized. "I'm sure my father would like you to come, too. He seems to regard you as another daughter," he said, trying to add weight to his invitation. He waited for that to sink in before saying anything more. Overkill was just as bad as neglecting to say anything at all.

At the mention of his father, Destiny allowed herself a small smile. Glancing over her shoulder to make sure the man was still in the other room, she said, "Your father's a very nice man."

"Well, we agree on that," Logan told her.

And more than likely on very little else, Destiny added silently.

With a preoccupied nod, she began to leave the apartment. She'd let Sean do his work. If she felt there was anything to add, she still had the key to Paula's apartment in her pocket. She could come back at a later date, when there was no one to get in her way.

Her hand on the doorknob, Logan's question made her pause in midstep.

"You want someone to take you home?"

Was he treating her like a civilian? Or did he just assume that she'd locked down her hysteria and was just a tiny step away from having a complete meltdown?

Turning to face the younger Cavanaugh, she looked at him, not exactly certain just how to interpret what he'd just said.

"What?"

"Would you like an officer to take you home?" he asked her, tendering the offer with a smile. "I'd offer to take you home myself, but I seem to be a little tied up at the moment."

He was serious. Either he was being too kind—or too cynical and doubting her actual feelings. She wasn't sure which bothered her more.

"Why would you think that I'd need someone to take me home?" she asked.

Why did she take everything as a challenge to her authority? He was trying to be understanding. Obviously that was wasted on this woman. "Well, you did just have a big shock."

"I'm not going home," she told him. Not wanting to explain herself any more than she absolutely had to, Destiny walked out.

"Are you going to be all right?" Sean asked as she passed him.

Sean's concern, at least, she didn't have to wonder about. She knew it was genuine and smiled with gratitude.

"Yes," she told him, not wanting the man to worry about her. He had enough to deal with these days. He didn't need her to burden him. Besides, she wasn't about to share her pain with him or with anyone. That was hers and hers alone to deal with.

And the way to deal with it was to keep busy.

She wasn't going home right now, even though the hour grew late. Home was just a medium-size shell that she got to rattle around in, waiting for the beginning of her next workday.

And, since technically she wasn't supposed to be working this case on the city's dime, she had to do it on her own time. That meant going into the lab and the small cubbyhole that comprised her "office" during something other than her regular work hours.

As in now.

She took the elevator down to the ground floor. It went straight down without a stop. Getting off, she walked directly to the double outer doors and pushed them open. The night air was chilly and damp as it greeted her.

Destiny drew in a deep breath and then another, trying to make herself come around.

With renewed purpose and borrowed energy, she walked briskly from the entrance to the apartment building to the curb where she'd parked her car.

And then she stopped dead.

There was no way she was going anywhere. Some jerk had double-parked his car parallel to hers and was completely blocking her exit.

She was stuck.

Biting back a barrage of less than flattering words that leaped to her lips, Destiny peered into the offending vehicle, trying to see if she could ascertain what kind of village idiot belonged to the car.

That was when she saw the official markings. And the communications radio that was mounted beneath the dashboard.

A standard Crown Victoria, the white car was an unmarked police vehicle. And she had a really strong hunch she knew whom it belonged to.

Chapter 4

When he heard the elevator opening, Logan automatically looked in that direction. He was surprised to see Destiny getting off.

"Forget something?" he asked, raising his voice in order to be heard.

Canvassing the floor, he was clear down the hall from the elevator. So far, he'd had next to no luck getting anyone to answer, despite the hour.

The only door that had opened so far had been by a very grumpy older man in a stained T-shirt and rumpled trousers of an indeterminable color. Both items of clothing looked as if the man had slept in them for at least the past year.

The man also, when questioned, didn't seem to speak any English. Whatever language he did speak, Logan was entirely unfamiliar with it. He was fluent in Spanish and knew a handful of other languages well enough to at least identify what they were. The old man was muttering at him in what he could only guess was an offshoot of some Slavic language, definitely not Russian in origin.

Thanking the man, Logan went to the next door. And the next.

So far, no one else had answered, but he'd canvassed only a quarter of the floor before his father's chief assistant had stepped off the elevator again.

"No, I didn't forget anything," Destiny retorted, irritated because she wanted to be on her way already, "but I think you did."

Logan cocked his head and eyed her, the person who might or might not be behind the next door temporarily forgotten. He watched as she walked toward him, appreciating the subtle sway of her hips. She was one of those people who was totally unaware of just how stunning she was.

But it wasn't lost on him.

She didn't seem like the type to play games, especially not at a time like this, so whatever she was referring to had to be on the level. The problem was, he had absolutely no idea what that was.

"Come again?" he finally said.

"You double-park your car downstairs?" she asked pointedly.

"No. Yeah," he amended in the next breath, remembering.

His automatic response was "no" because as a rule, he never double-parked. Aside from it being against the rules, he liked his car, and that was a good way to get it nicked and dinged. But this evening he'd made an exception because there'd been no spots and he thought he'd be finished and out in no time. But he'd obviously miscalculated.

"That was your car I blocked?" he asked incredulously. Wow, what were the odds?

"That was—and still is—my car," she told him. Why wasn't he moving? "Could you come down please and move your car?" It really wasn't a request.

Logan could see that begging a couple of minutes' indulgence, until he was at least finished with this side of the floor, was just *not* going to fly in this case. So he dropped his hand away from the door he'd been knocking on, nodded and said, "Sure," just as the door in front of him opened.

This time, the responding tenant was definitely *not* a rumpled, grumpy old man. It was a barefoot blonde wearing the tightest cutoff denim shorts he'd ever seen. The white T-shirt she had on told him that she didn't believe in bras.

"Yes?" she asked in a small, soft voice. She looked from him to Destiny and then back again, making no secret of the fact that she preferred talking to men.

Holding up his badge and police ID, Logan flashed what one of his sisters referred to as his "bone melting" smile at the woman in apartment 3D.

"Detective Cavanaugh with the Aurora P.D., ma'am. I need to ask you a few questions, but first I have to tend to something else. I'll be right back, I promise," he said, sounding as sincere as a preacher on Sunday. He held up his index finger as if that somehow reinforced the fact that he wanted her to just hold on for a few minutes until he could get back to her.

"What's this about?" the woman asked, calling after him as he walked into the elevator right behind Destiny.

"I'll explain everything in five minutes," he called back, raising his voice as the elevator door slid closed, cutting him off from the blonde. "Sorry about the car," he told Destiny, turning his attention to her and never missing a beat. "I thought I wasn't going to be here long."

"I guess it's a night for surprises," Destiny quipped dryly, saying the words more to herself than to him.

But something in her voice managed to catch his attention. As the stainless-steel door opened and she stepped out, Logan caught her by the elbow before she could get too far.

Startled, she turned to look at him quizzically. Now what?

"Do you have anyone?" he asked her.

No, not anymore. The words seemed to echo in her head, draining her soul. Shaking it off, she stared at him.

"What?" she demanded.

"Do you have anyone to talk to?" he elaborated. "Someone to stay with or to have them come over and stay with you?"

Destiny raised her chin, the barricade she kept around herself growing a little higher. "Look, I'm not exactly sure what you're asking, but I don't need a baby-sitter."

That meant the answer was no, Logan thought. The woman had already said that her sister was her only living kin. With her gone, that left no one to call family. He had no idea what that was like. All of his life, from his very first memory, he'd always had siblings and cousins, and now that he knew he was a Cavanaugh, he had enough relatives to populate a small city.

Despite the fact that there were times he felt as if he would have traded his soul for some privacy, for an island of time alone with his thoughts and away from well-meaning relatives, he knew that if he had to endure that on a full-time, daily basis, it would have eaten away at him.

"I didn't say that you did," he told her, his voice low-key. "But if you want to wait around for a bit while I finish knocking on these doors to see if there's anyone willing to talk and tell me if they saw or heard something, maybe we could go out afterwards, catch a cup of coffee. Talk," he emphasized. The elevator stopped. A moment later, as if it first had to pause, the door to the lobby opened.

She walked out of the building's glass doors ahead of Logan. Her first thought was that he was hitting on her, but that cocky expression she'd noticed earlier on his face was absent. And to give him his due, he did sound sincere. Since he was Sean's son and she dearly loved the man, she gave Logan the benefit of the doubt. After all, since he *was* Sean's son, maybe a little compassion had rubbed off on him.

She realized, in a moment of weakness, that she appreciated the offer. But that still didn't mean that she wanted him hovering around her, possibly witnessing her break down.

"I'm not going to do anything stupid or drastic," she assured Logan.

Logan shrugged as if that had never crossed his mind. "I'm just in the mood for some decent coffee. By definition that means not the kind that comes in a paper cup," he told her.

She'd never been discerning about her coffee. As long as it was black and hot, that was all that she required.

"I'll be fine," she insisted, then softened a little as she added, "But thanks."

"No problem," he murmured. He caught himself wondering, just for a split second, what she was like without all that barbed wire around her.

She watched him get into his vehicle. A moment later, he turned his ignition key and the car came to life. With his eyes all but glued to the rearview mirror, he eased his car out slowly, going backward one inch at a time. Traffic was light at the moment, but that was subject to instant change, even at this hour of the evening.

Clearing her vehicle, he pulled up the handbrake. Logan allowed his engine to idle as he waited for her to get into her car and pull it out of its current parking spot.

"I'll take a rain check," Destiny impulsively called out through the open passenger side window just before she peeled out of the spot and seamlessly merged into the flow of cars.

She didn't stop until she came to the next light. It

was red, but the color barely registered with her brain in time.

She was too busy upbraiding herself.

A rain check? What the hell had possessed her to say that? Was it just to establish some kind of connection with another human being, subconsciously comforting herself with the knowledge that she didn't have to be alone if she didn't choose to be? That she could establish some kind of contact with another human being anytime she wanted to? And that if she was alone, it was because she *chose* to be that way.

Words, she was playing with words.

It didn't make the empty, gnawing feeling in the pit of her stomach go away.

She vacillated between being numb and being shattered.

"Oh, Paula," she murmured under her breath, blinking back hot tears. "What did you go and leave yourself open to?"

No matter what the answer to that was, if her sister had openly invited her killer into the apartment or the person had let himself in with a copy of her key, Paula was still dead.

She was still not coming back.

Paula had always been a delicate, small-boned little thing, and even if she hadn't been drugged, she wouldn't have been able to fight her attacker off if he had been any larger than a small field mouse.

"I tried to get you to take self-defense classes," Destiny angrily shouted into the emptiness, the feeling of helplessness snowballing into outrage and fury. "Why didn't you listen to me? Why the hell didn't you *ever* listen to anything I said to you?"

It seemed to her as if, up until these past two years, anytime she'd made a constructive suggestion, Paula would turn around and do the exact opposite.

And yet, she knew her sister had always loved her. Loved her as fiercely as she loved Paula.

A lot of good that did either of them now, Destiny thought sadly.

With a sigh, she stepped on the gas.

One Police Plaza looked mournful silhouetted against the dark, moonless sky. The building had a minimum of lights on, beneath which a handful of detectives were burning the midnight oil, trying to solve a case or just tying up the loose ends on one.

A slightly lesser complement of officers patrolled the streets now than during the daylight hours. She didn't know if that was a good thing or a bad thing.

Parking her vehicle near the building, Destiny got out and began to hurry up the ten stone steps.

What she was really doing, she knew, was trying to outrun the loneliness inside her. She was having little success at that.

The only way she would be able to get through this, Destiny told herself, was to find Paula's killer and make him pay.

"Damn it, Paula, you should have told me who you were dating."

Maybe the guy wasn't responsible for what had ultimately happened, but at least it would have been a start, someone to question so she could begin putting the disjointed pieces together.

The last phrase echoed in her head. *Begin putting the disjointed pieces together.*

Well, if she didn't have Paula's mystery man's name, she would have to start somewhere else to make this puzzle come together.

Destiny suddenly thought of the prescription bottle that Logan had found in the medicine cabinet. Now that she thought about it, the whole thing just didn't seem to ring true to her. It didn't seem like Paula.

Granted her sister did have a lot of trouble sleeping and she had taken the drug when it had first come out. But Paula was stubborn. She would have never allowed herself to be dependent on a drug. Most likely, she would have tried her best to use the prescription as little as possible.

Now that she thought about it, she remembered that Paula was adamantly against taking drugs of any kind. This even went so far as to include simple painkillers. She wouldn't take them even when she had one of her excruciating headaches.

She and Paula had argued over that more than once. But Paula wouldn't be budged. Her deep aversion came from the fact that her best friend in high school had had a drug problem. A week before her graduation, the girl, Rachel Wyman, had accidentally overdosed. She was dead before she ever reached the hospital.

Paula had been the one to find her.

Just like I was the one who found you, Destiny thought ruefully.

That was when Paula started getting involved in anti-drug campaigns, volunteering her time and considerable artistic talents to do whatever she could to try to save someone else from ending up the way that Rachel had.

So, feeling that way, what was Paula doing with a brand-new prescription for sleeping pills?

Making a decision, Destiny turned on her heel and hurried back to her car. Blessed with what amounted to total recall, she had the ability to remember anything that had crossed her line of vision.

Right now, as she concentrated, she remembered the name of the pharmacy that was written across the top of the bottle.

She also remembered the prescription number on the bottle, a long fourteen-digit number. What she hadn't noted at the time, because she'd been so focused on keeping herself together, was the prescribing doctor's name. She wanted to speak to him because, as a rule, her sister didn't go to doctors.

The pharmacist on duty expressed an initial reluctance to answer her questions about her sister's medication until Destiny flashed her badge and ID for him. Mentally, she crossed her fingers that the young pharmacist wasn't the belt-and-suspenders type. Because if he was, she had the sinking feeling that he would have felt compelled not just to take note of her ID but to call in and verify with her superior whether or not she was really supposed to be there, asking questions.

Destiny held her breath until the pharmacist finally lifted his rather thin, sloping shoulders, then dropped them again in what amounted to a disinterested shrug. With that, he went to the computer to access the prescription in question.

After several minutes had passed and the pharmacist still hadn't stopped searching, Destiny felt compelled to ask, "Is there anything wrong?"

"That depends on your point of view," he told her. His brow furrowed in frustration. "I can't seem to find that prescription number. Are you sure that you got the numbers down right?"

There were a great many things that she was uncertain about, but that didn't include her ability to recall things in crystal clarity. "Positive," she told the pharmacist.

The young man frowned, his thin lips all but disappearing. "What did you say the patient's name was again?"

"Paula Richardson," she repeated, then recited, "Her date of birth is oh-three, oh-six, nineteen eighty-six." Taking a breath to help steel herself off, she said, "She was found dead today."

Startled, the pharmacist immediately asked, "And you think that the prescription was responsible? I assure you, every chemical used is of the highest grade. It couldn't have been our—"

She held up her hand to stop him. When she spoke, it was in the small, soothing voice she'd once used to chase away Paula's nightmares.

"No one is accusing your pharmacy of anything. We're just trying to gather as much information as we can right now."

Temporarily placated, the pharmacist returned to his computer. Hitting the keyboard, he scrolled down several pages.

"Well, she's here in our records—we filled a standard antibiotic for her at the beginning of the year. Amoxicillin. For the flu," he said, still staring at the screen. He hit several keys that took him back and forth between a couple of screens. "Nope, no sleeping pills," he verified. "You're sure that was her name was on the bottle?"

"Yes, I'm sure." Her mouth curved for a second in a semblance of a smile, doing her best to silently reassure the man that no one at the pharmacy was in trouble. She had the information she needed. "Thanks for your help."

He seemed a little confused. "But I didn't find anything."

No, on the contrary, you did, Destiny thought. The pharmacist with the baby face had indirectly found that someone had gone to a great deal of trouble and had carefully staged her sister's death scene. The person had even gone to the trouble of replicating a prescription medication.

That meant that someone had *planned* to kill her sister. Had actually targeted Paula.

But why?

And to what end?

This didn't sound like the work of an obsessive serial killer, because there were too many details adhered to. Besides, as a rule of thumb, a serial killer didn't try to make a murder victim look like someone who committed suicide. Covertly or blatantly, serial killers were usually quite proud of their sick handiwork and enjoyed showing it off. Enjoyed basking in splashy headlines. At the same time, they usually were daring law enforcement agents to try to catch them.

This had been covered up, its sole purpose appearing to have been to kill Paula.

Again, *why?*

It was half an hour later and she was back mentally staring at that question. And back driving toward the police station.

With this new information, there were things she needed to check out, to look into. The precinct was the only place she knew of with the kind of wealth of information and access to that information that she needed.

The precinct parking lot looked almost emptier this time than it had just a little while ago. Blocking the effects, Destiny hurried up the stairs for a second time, eager to get started. Eager to get to her desk.

She needed to document what she'd discovered. In the morning, she'd get in touch with Cavanaugh—she assumed the good-looking detective would be the one to work her sister's case—and let him know that the prescription he'd found in the medicine cabinet and felt went a long way in supporting his suicide theory didn't belong to her sister.

It belonged, in one way or another, to the killer. The prescription number, when she'd finally prevailed upon the pharmacist to look through the pharmacy chain's archives, had once been the number on a bottle of cough medicine that had been prescribed for a child with bronchitis.

She couldn't help wondering if there was some obscure connection there. Tracking down the name on the actual prescription would be her first order of business, she decided.

Armed with coffee from the vending machine and her determination, Destiny got off the elevator when it came to a stop and opened in the basement. Trying to think only of making progress and not about her sister, she made her way down the winding corridor to her office.

It never occurred to her that she might fail in reaching her objective. Because, as the popular saying she believed with all her heart went, failure was not an option here. She wouldn't allow it to be.

Chapter 5

"So, Dad, how's it going?"

Walking into the newly redecorated, state-of-the-art criminology lab at the ungodly hour of 7:00 a.m. the next morning, Logan crossed to the middle of the room. His father stood over a table that was rivaled only by the enormous one in Andrew Cavanaugh's dining room.

The head of the crime lab was busy testing the contents of some substance Logan wasn't even going to try to identify.

Wearing his white lab coat, Sean glanced up to see his son approaching. Surprised, he looked over Logan's head at the clock on the wall behind him.

Well, this was unusual.

"You're in early," he commented. Logan was the one they used to have to dynamite out of bed to get him to school on time. As far as he knew, his son still loved sleeping in. *Early* was not a word Logan regarded with any semblance of approval. "Something to do with the case?"

Logan moved his shoulders in a vague shrug. "In a manner of speaking, I guess, but I wasn't asking you about the evidence just now."

Still working, Sean raised a quizzical eyebrow in response. "Oh?"

"No," Logan told him, "I was asking you 'personally' how it was going."

"Fine." There was a note of amused caution in Sean's voice. Then, because he did possess a measure of curiosity and Logan was behaving rather strangely, Sean pressed for details. "Are you asking about anything specifically—personally?" he tacked on, deliberately highlighting the word Logan had used.

Oh, the hell with it. He might as well just blurt it out, Logan decided. "Kenny said that you and Matt's mother are seeing each other," he said, referring to his sister, Kendra. "Regularly," he added in case his father was going to try to pretend not to know what he was talking about. "I just wanted to ask how that was going."

So, that was it. Sean had wondered how long it would take for word to spread. Apparently not very long at all. The Cavanaugh grapevine seemed to have an even faster connection than the Cavelli grapevine did.

"Sabrina Abilene and I are more than 'seeing' each other, Logan," he informed his son, doing his best to sound serious and keep the laughter at bay.

Logan sighed dramatically, leaned his hip against the long, sleek stainless-steel table that displayed a host of mysterious instruments and said to his father in a low, serious voice, "Well, young man, I think it's time that we had 'The Talk.'"

Sean laughed then, affectionately cuffing the back of his son's head the way he'd sometimes done when Logan and his brothers were younger and had been guilty of doing something stupid.

"That's enough out of you, or there'll be some serious consequences, Detective Cavanaugh. Go, make yourself useful." He pointed toward the door. "Do some detective work and earn that big, hefty salary the city's paying you."

"That only takes about two hours out of my day."

If he looked at his pay and divided it by the number of hours he put in overall, he was getting paid a pittance. But he wasn't in it for the money, or even because it was the family business. He believed in his work. Believed in making a difference. But that wasn't anything he wanted to advertise. It clashed with his devil-may-care image.

Nodding toward what his father was testing, he asked, "You find anything new?"

"Nothing we haven't already surmised. Paula Richardson had enough sleeping pills in her system to put a school of sharks to sleep. The slashed wrists were just overkill. Too bad. She looked like a lovely girl."

"A lovely girl somebody really wanted dead," Logan commented. "How's your chief assistant holding up?"

Sean smiled, noting how hard Logan was trying to appear as if he was completely detached in his view of the case and Destiny's connection to it. If Logan had really been detached, Sean mused, he wouldn't have felt the need to have that point driven home.

"On the surface, she's behaving very professionally. But I won't pretend that I'm not concerned about her, Logan. She's keeping everything bottled up inside, and that kind of thing can only be sustained for so long before the inner pressure gets to be too much. Keep an eye out on her for me, will you?"

Logan was surprised by the request. "Dad, I'm going to be working the case, remember?"

"Yeah, well, so will she, no matter what anyone says to the contrary." He smiled to himself. "She's stubborn enough to be one of us," he told his son. "By the way, she went by the pharmacy where the prescription was issued."

Logan was about to protest that he had kept the prescription container in his possession, dropping it off at the lab last night, but that obviously hadn't made a difference.

"And?"

"And it turns out that they never issued the prescription to our victim. They have a file on her and the number came out of their pharmacy, but years ago and not for sleeping pills but for some cough medicine for a little girl. Backs up Destiny's theory that her sister was murdered. By the way," he added mildly, "her desk is at the other end of the floor—in case you want to swing by sometime and, you know, exchange theories," he concluded euphemistically.

Logan merely shook his head. "You know, Dad, if I

didn't know better, I'd say you had something up your sleeve."

Sean innocently raised one hand into the air, demonstrating. "Just my arm, boy. Just my arm."

It was a well-known fact, especially around his family, that people in love tended to want to pair up everyone else in the firm belief that *everyone* should be as happy as they were.

Standing in the doorway, Logan took a good look at his father, seeing him in a completely different light since when he had first entered.

"Dad?"

Sean was already refocused on his task. His "Yes?" was more than a little distracted.

The thought of his father in a romantic relationship had never really crossed his mind before. He wasn't certain how to react, really. But he and his siblings had always been cautioned about leaping to conclusions, so he decided to ask first before trying to get used to the idea.

"You're not in love or anything, are you?"

"Define 'or anything,'" Sean countered, amused by the question. When his son seemed at a loss for words, Sean told him. "You'll be the second to know when and if I am," he promised.

"Who'll be the first?" Logan asked suspiciously. He fully expected his father to say "Sabrina."

But again, his father surprised him. "Me," Sean replied simply.

Logan left the lab, feeling more than a little bewildered even if he didn't show it. His world had been turned upside down. First they had discovered that his father had been accidentally switched at birth with another male infant and that he, and thus *they,* were actually part of the Cavanaugh family. If that wasn't enough, now it looked as if after years of being content to be their sole parent, his father was dating.

Seriously dating, from the sound of it.

At twenty-eight, Logan felt he was too old to be entertaining the idea of getting a stepmother. Wasn't that something children acquired?

You're not the one who matters here.

That was just plain weird, he thought. He could almost hear Bridget's voice in his head. Bridget, the one who always put him in his place.

The main thing to remember, he told himself, was that his father seemed happy, and heaven only knew his father *deserved* to be happy.

Arriving at the closed elevator door, he was about to press the button on the wall beside it when a light pooling along the floor down the hall caught his eye, and then his attention. He'd come in early to catch his father alone so that he could feel him out about the woman he was seeing—he'd run into Kendra and Matt on his way out of the precinct last night and they had mentioned the change in his father's evening schedule. Logan knew his father was always in early and always alone, which made it a good time to talk to him.

Was he wrong? Did his father have a kindred spirit amid the CSI unit?

Curious, Logan moved away from the elevator bank and made his way down the hallway.

He had a hunch the light was coming from Destiny's

office even before he actually got to the doorway and looked in. Given the current case the unit and he had just caught, her being here early didn't exactly come as a great shock to him.

But it did surprise him that Destiny appeared to be wearing the same clothes she'd had on yesterday.

"Didn't you go home last night?" he asked.

Completely absorbed by what she was doing, Destiny jumped at the sound of Logan's deep voice intruding into her world. She pressed her lips together just in time to suppress the yelp of surprise that automatically rose to her tongue.

Taking in a shaky breath as she tried to calm her nerves, Destiny turned her chair halfway toward the doorway to confirm what she already knew. That Logan was standing there.

She shrugged in vague dismissal. "I lost track of time."

There was something extremely attractive about the rumpled way she looked, he thought. He found himself wishing that they weren't involved professionally so he'd be free to get involved another way. "Then let me clue you in—it's tomorrow."

She frowned. Why was he even here at this hour? "Just what everyone needs, a talking desk calendar. Thank you, your work here is done," she said, hoping he would leave so she could concentrate.

"And so will you be if you don't go home and get some rest."

Her frown deepened. Was that a note of concern she heard in his voice?

No, she was just tired, that's all. And then she remembered his offer of coffee and to listen if she just wanted to talk. Maybe he really was being nice and she was being too hard on him because her temper had shortened by half. Lack of sleep tended to do that to her, to make her irritable and impatient.

"I'll rest when we catch the bastard who did this," she told him.

"Your sister wouldn't want you running yourself into the ground like this," he pointed out.

Now that was just empty talk. He didn't even know her sister—and now he never would, she thought with a pang before she could tamp down the pain. With effort, she firmly put her emotions under lock and key. Anything she couldn't use to help her catch Paula's killer would just need to wait.

"My sister didn't want me doing a lot of things," she pointed out briskly. "She wasn't the easiest person to get along with."

Logan had a feeling his father's chief assistant was using anger to keep herself from falling apart. Whatever worked. With a smile, he made an observation. "She probably said the same thing about you."

"Yeah, she did." Logan had expected her to admit as much. The half smile that accompanied the words, though, was a surprise.

It was the first time he'd seen her *really* smile. It was a nice smile and not one of those smirky, snarky smiles that had a person bracing for some sort of witty, biting put-down. Hers was a sunrise-type smile that brought warmth with it. Definitely lit up the recipient, he realized, charmed.

"You know, you're really not supposed to be working on this," he reminded her tactfully.

He was aware that his father wouldn't take her to task for this. He'd already demonstrated as much. But the homicide lieutenant who had put him on this case, he was a different story. He liked things by the book. So had he, Logan thought—when he was twelve. Now, solving cases was more of an improvisational theater at work. He made things up as he went along, and when it worked it was fantastic.

Destiny pointed to the square silver clock on the opposite wall. "I start work at nine. This is still before my workday." Her eyes narrowed as she looked at him and dug in. She really couldn't seem to concentrate with him here. It was as if he was eating up her oxygen and making the room very, very warm. "Anything else?"

He remembered what his father had just mentioned. "Yeah. Did you find anything else besides the fact that the prescription with her name on it didn't really belong to your sister?" he asked. Then, because his question had caught her off guard, he added, "I stopped to talk to my father this morning. He filled me in."

She just naturally assumed that meant that Logan had stopped by the lab to check on the progress being made on the case. Why else would he be here? She had to admit that the detective's thoroughness took her by surprise. Cavanaugh or not, she wouldn't have thought that Logan was that dedicated to his job. He hadn't given her that kind of an impression when she'd spoken with him yesterday.

For once it was nice to discover she was wrong.

"Yes, actually, I did find out something." And then she raised her eyes to his and qualified, "I think."

"That sleeping with your head on your desk will give you a pretty bad crick in your neck?" he guessed.

"Besides that," she told him. She turned her monitor so that he had a better view of the screen. "I think I found a pattern," she said excitedly.

Actually, there was no "think" about it. Destiny *knew* she had. The cases, all appearing to be singular in nature, were far too similar to one another for this to be some unhappy coincidence occurring again and again—especially since there had been five other cases in as many years.

"What kind of a pattern?" Logan asked, looking at her rather than at the screen.

"The kind of pattern that involves apparent "suicides" of attractive young women ranging between the ages of twenty-one and thirty-five who, according to the police files, killed themselves after breaking up with—or being dumped by—a mysterious boyfriend whom their family and friends not only didn't get to meet, but didn't even know by name." Finished, she looked at him again. "Sound familiar?"

Sounded identical, he thought, but he was never one to get ahead of himself on a case. "If they were called suicides, why were there police reports filed?" he asked.

That was a good point—and she had an equally good answer. She'd known the only way to sell this was to stay one step ahead of Logan. "Because in all the cases, someone in the family didn't think that it was suicide, that the so-called mysterious boyfriend did it." She stopped for a second, straightening and pulling her shoulders back so that a minor cracking noise was heard, like the salute of old-fashioned cap pistols going off one at a time.

"They're all open cases," she informed him, sitting back now. "In each case there was not enough evidence to lead them to a suspect." And then she frowned slightly as she leaned back in her chair and rocked. "I didn't think so in the beginning, but it looks like we might have a serial killer on our hands. Or at the very least, a killer with an agenda."

Logan studied the last screen she'd pulled up. The details there were very close to matching the ones that had come up last night. Very slowly, he nodded.

"It looks like you might have something there." And then he smiled at her. "Nice work, Richardson. I'll take it from here."

The nascent smile vanished. "No, you won't," she countered with feeling.

"Look, I don't want any of the credit, but you know you're not supposed to be involved in this. It's a conflict of interest."

The hell it was. "I don't have any 'interest' to conflict," she shot back. "All I want is to help find Paula's killer—and apparently the killer of a lot of other innocent women, as well," she added, pointing to the monitor. "I don't have anyone to 'pin' this on, so it's not like

I have an agenda or anything. The only agenda I have is to solve this."

He wasn't going to leave her office without agreeing to let her work the case. She didn't care if she had to bodily restrain him. The thought brought an unexpected flash of heat with it that she quickly dismissed.

"Look," she argued, "I've already been a help. I found out that the prescription wasn't filled under my sister's name despite what the label said and I found all these other so-called suicides that match Paula's killer's M.O. Who knows what else I can find out if I go on working this?" she pushed.

"You don't have to convince me," he told her.

It was the brass she would be going up against, not him. After talking to her, after seeing her at work, he wasn't about to be a stickler about rules and regulations. He fully sympathized with what she was going through right now. In his opinion, finding her sister like that was an absolute living nightmare. Solving the case might actually give her sweet dreams. At the very least, it would give her the night back.

Besides, the woman was damn easy on the eyes, and she did keep him up on his toes. It would definitely be simpler to join forces than have to fight her.

"Well, then my working the case is a go, because you're the only one I care about right now." When she saw the grin slip over his lips, she knew she hadn't worded her answer to him correctly. A bright pink hue took her cheeks prisoner. Just in time for him to see.

"Wait," she cried, determined to straighten this out. "That didn't come out right."

"Came out fine from where I'm standing," Logan told her. And then he sighed. He wasn't going to even pretend to stand in her way. He didn't belong with the establishment, only the rebels. "Okay, keep at it. I know my dad's not about to come down on you. He completely understands the idea of family loyalty—"

"Do you?" she heard herself asking, realizing that she wanted to hear a positive answer out of him.

He watched her for a long moment, green eyes meeting blue. And, for the briefest of seconds, soul touching soul. "Yeah," he heard himself saying quietly, "I do."

"Good," she said so softly he read the words on her lips more than heard them. "Then I'll just get back to work and touch base with you later."

"Later," he echoed as he walked away.

Part of him had an uneasy feeling that he was getting in over his head here, but there was nothing he could do about it.

The other part was damn well looking forward to it.

Chapter 6

"Damn it!" Lieutenant Bailey's disgruntled voice greeted Logan even before he crossed the threshold into the squad room.

This, Logan thought, did not sound good.

Usually it took a few hours before the day began to look as if it was going to hell. Having it begin in hell guaranteed a slow, unmerciful torture for him. When Lieutenant Bailey wasn't happy, *no one* in his squad was happy.

Walking in, Logan saw the reason why the lieutenant's voice had carried so well. The man was not in his office. Right now, he was standing near the doorway, talking on his cell. Or rather, the older, disgruntled-looking man was cursing into his phone.

"Problem, Lieutenant?" he asked mildly as the other

man abruptly disconnected the call that was apparently creating his less than jovial mood.

"Only if you call working with half a squad a problem. That was Wakefield, calling in sick. This is worse than when we had the blue flu," he grumbled, referring to an incident several years back. At that time, an inordinate number of the uniformed officers called in sick in protest over what they felt was a wrongful disciplinary action of one of their own. Now that he recalled, Brian Cavanaugh had looked into the matter, found the charges to be false and had all actions dropped.

"Nearly half of my men are out sick," the lieutenant bit off in frustration. "I just hope the crazies don't start coming out of the woodwork." He looked at Logan as if seeing him for the first time. "You close that suicide case that came in last night?"

"Funny thing about that, Lieutenant."

Bailey's dark eyes grew even darker as he glared at him over his hawklike, patrician nose. "You're not going to tell me that wasn't a suicide, are you?"

Logan ignored the warning note in the lieutenant's voice. He didn't believe in hiding information. The man needed to be kept in the loop, at least to some extent. "Well, yeah, actually I am," Logan told him, then quickly added, "But there's more," before Bailey could unleash his mercurial temper.

"More?" The lieutenant stared at him in disbelief. "What kind of 'more'?" he asked.

Logan knew what he was about to say wouldn't be welcome, but in this case, he found himself agreeing with Destiny. "It looks like this might be the work of a serial killer."

Bailey sank down in Sullivan's chair. "Aw, hell, no."

Taking a seat behind his own desk, Logan nodded. "I'm afraid so."

It took less than a minute for Bailey to rally. He was back in fighting form and ready to issue a challenge. "Who the hell says it's a serial killer?" he demanded angrily.

Logan was about to say that it was the victim's sister, but then decided it sounded better if he fell back on Destiny's title at the crime lab instead. If nothing else, it carried some weight.

"One of the CSIs. The head of the day shift's chief assistant," he said, deliberately not referring to him as his father. He and his siblings had all earned their present positions, and the less attention paid to the fact that their father was the head of the crime lab, the better for everyone all around. "She found five other open, suspicious 'suicide' cases that had far too many similarities to this case to just shrug off and pass over."

"And you looked these cases over and agreed?" Bailey pressed.

"I haven't had a chance yet," Logan told him truthfully. "But I was just about to do that." As he talked, Logan turned on his computer. It took the machine several seconds to respond and come to life.

"All right, you do that." Bailey sounded exasperated as he issued the order. Rising to his feet, he nodded at the desk he'd just vacated. "When's Sullivan supposed to be coming back?"

The wedding had taken place only last weekend. The lieutenant had been invited but hadn't attended. Unlike Brian Cavanaugh, he didn't believe in socializing with his men.

"Not for another week and a half," Logan answered.

The news was not well received. Bailey's frown intensified.

"Well, I can't give you anyone else from the squad. Half of them are out sick and the other half are up to their ears in unsolved cases. This month's stats are going straight to hell."

"The chief assistant offered to work with me on this one—if it's okay with you, Lieutenant," Logan added.

As a rule, he preferred to ask forgiveness rather than permission, but seeing as how this was right out in front of him and the lieutenant was bemoaning the lack of bodies to do the work, Logan decided that this might be the better approach.

Bailey sighed. It was a known fact that the man wasn't much on accepting outside help. He preferred the "glory," as he referred to it, to remain within the department. But in this case, he had no choice. They needed to close some of the cases. After a moment, he nodded.

"Desperate times require desperate measures, I guess. All right. Use whatever resources are offered," he said, and Logan had the distinct impression that the man was blatantly hinting that he could turn to the chief of D's if it proved necessary.

"Oh, and one more thing—I don't want this going out to the media until I give the okay. The last damn thing we need right now is for the public to start panicking and seeing a serial killer behind every building." Bailey's penetrating gaze met Logan's. "Understood?"

Translation, the lieutenant doesn't want to look as if he's not doing his job.

Logan had always thought that bringing the public in was a good thing. For every thousand crazies who called in with dead-end tips, they'd get one really good, valid one that enabled them to nab their perpetrators a lot quicker.

But this was the lieutenant's call. "Understood," Logan answered.

"Good."

The conversation over, the lieutenant marched back into his office, looking like the very personification of a disgruntled man who had far too much on his plate.

Logan waited until Bailey was out of earshot, then he picked up his telephone receiver and called the extension in Destiny's office. Detail oriented, he'd taken note of the number when he'd walked into her office.

The phone rang a total of four times. He was just about to hang up, thinking that she must have stepped away from her area, when he heard the phone pick up.

"Crime lab."

The voice sounded preoccupied, as if he'd interrupted her. "Destiny?"

There was a slight hesitation, as if she was surprised that anyone would recognize her voice. "Yes?"

"This is Cavanaugh. Logan," he added since there were so many of them. "Good news—"

"I know who you are," she cut in. "I recognized your

voice." What she hadn't liked was that not only did she recognize his voice, but her pulse had jumped when she heard it. Maybe she was just sleep deprived and not just reacting to his resonant and sexy voice. "What good news?" she asked, trying not to let herself anticipate anything and not quite succeeding. "Did you find who did this to Paula?"

"Not that good," he qualified.

"Then what is it?" she asked impatiently.

"My lieutenant just said that in light of the fact that my partner's on his honeymoon and half the detectives up here are out with the flu, he officially okayed the two of us working together for the time being."

She had learned to take most everything with a grain of salt and a great deal of caution. "Does your lieutenant know who I—"

"No, he doesn't, and I purposely didn't mention you by name, only by your title."

"By my title?" she questioned. She didn't think he was even aware of that.

"Yeah, you know, chief assistant to the crime lab's head of the day shift." That was quite a mouthful to get right. "Right now, that seemed to be good enough for the lieutenant. He said because we're so shorthanded up here, you and I should work together on this case— at least until Sully gets back."

"Sully?" she echoed. Who or what was a "Sully"?

"Yeah." And then he gave her his partner's full name. "Detective Eric Sullivan. He's on his honeymoon at the moment and isn't due to be back for another week and a half."

She'd take whatever she could get. "That gives us a little leeway," she commented.

"Yeah," he agreed. Who was she kidding? The woman wasn't nearly as laid-back about this as she was trying to portray. "Oh, and one more thing—"

There was always just "one more thing," she thought. She could feel her shoulders stiffening as she braced herself. "And that is?"

"The lieutenant wants this kept from the media for as long as possible. He said he doesn't want single women to be afraid to go out in the evening."

"The serial killer doesn't kill his victims in the street," she pointed out, adding grimly, "He apparently kills his victims after he gets tired of them and dumps them."

"I kept that little detail from him," Logan told her. "I've come to the conclusion that the less I share with the lieutenant, the more leeway I have to work on a case."

"As in bringing me in and not telling him my last name," she surmised.

He didn't think that she was going to have any particular problem with that. "It's what you wanted, wasn't it?"

"Absolutely," she told him with feeling. It was just that by *not* telling his lieutenant her name, she felt as if they were actually lying to the man. And that could come back and bite them. "Don't think that I'm not grateful—" she began.

He cut her off right there. "We'll get to that later," he promised her with a definite grin in his voice, instinctively knowing that was going to distract her and get under her skin. He had a feeling that messing with her and getting her annoyed with him would focus the woman on solving the case and not on her personal loss.

"Okay, so how do you want to do this?" she asked.

"Do what?"

"Work together," she underscored. She felt a warmth creeping up her cheeks when she realized that he might have thought she was making a reference to something personal. More than likely he was probably more accustomed to that sort of thing than to working with a woman professionally. "Do you want me to come upstairs to you, or do you want to come down to me?"

He disliked having to rely on another computer, preferring to work on his own. Logan glanced toward Sully's desk. That was as good a place as any. Actually, now that he looked around, there were a good many empty desks in the immediate area. This flu thing really *was* taking its toll.

"A lot of detectives are out sick," he told her again. "So there's plenty of space up here." The crime lab had always struck him as rather claustrophobic, not to mention subterranean. "Might do you good to work aboveground for a change."

"I'm not exactly a gopher," she told him, picking up on his inference. "I go out in daylight on occasion." She didn't attempt to hide the note of sarcasm in her voice.

"Actually, I was thinking more along the lines of a vampire, not a gopher." When she made no response, he added, "You know, a creature of the night, that sort of thing."

"I know what a vampire is," she told him shortly.

Was this his attempt at humor? Or was he flirting in some strange, abstract way? Either way, he needed to stop it. This was a serious case they were working on. There was no time to waste on distractions. Her sister and a lot of other women were dead. They had to find the killer before he found another victim.

She blew out a breath, told herself to calm down and focus, then said, "I'll be up in a few minutes."

"Looking forward to it," he told her.

In response he heard a loud "click" in his ear. She'd hung up. Logan smiled to himself. Mission accomplished. He'd gotten her annoyed, he congratulated himself, and right now, "annoyed" was a lot better than "sad," which was what he'd picked up on in her voice earlier. And while the woman had every right to be sad, the emotion tended to paralyze a person. Annoyance, or its first cousin "anger," on the other hand, tended to light a fire under a person, which at the moment would serve them both a lot better than her being sad.

"Any particular place you want me?" Destiny asked ten minutes later. She'd come up carrying a large cardboard box filled with files, notebooks and miscellaneous information.

The expression on his face when Cavanaugh looked up told her that she'd made a tactical mistake with her wording. Again. What was it about this man that kept her tangling her words? She was seriously going to have to watch that. "To sit?" she added with emphasis, then repeated the question more fully. "Where do you want me to sit?"

"You can take Sully's desk. I don't know when the others are liable to come back, and there's no point in you having to play musical desks every morning, looking to see which is still unoccupied."

She deposited the cardboard box right in the middle of the desk and began to take out the files. Several looked thicker than he thought they should be, given that they'd only started their investigation.

Finished, she placed what appeared to be a jump drive on top of the files. The neat way they were stacked was in complete contrast to the rest of the desk, which overflowed with papers and folders. In truth, it looked as if the other detective had just stepped away from his desk to make a quick run to the vending machine, not a trip to Hawaii for the better part of two weeks.

Sitting down in the chair, Destiny found herself momentarily flustered when she discovered that her feet wouldn't reach the floor.

"Is your partner a giant?" she asked. Who would want their chair to be this high?

"Close," Logan allowed. He thought for a second, then said, "He's six-six." He watched as Destiny felt around along the bottom perimeter of the chair, looking for the height adjuster. "It's on the right," he told her. "The thing that adjusts your chair's height," he prompted.

"Oh. Thanks."

Finding the adjuster, she pressed hard and suddenly found herself dropping down, seat and all, like a stone.

The action jarred her, and it took a couple of moments for Destiny to start to feel all her individual parts back in working order.

"Don't mention it." His grin grew wider still. And more inviting. He had to be some lady-killer when he got going, she couldn't help thinking. That smile of his could definitely melt a rock at close range. "Anything I can do to help."

She merely nodded in response, not trusting herself to speak.

"Oh, and speaking of help…" he interjected, his voice deliberately trailing away.

"Yes?" she asked guardedly.

"As soon as you're settled in, I want to ask you a few questions," he told her.

What was it about this man that had her reacting so defensively? And heating so quickly? "What kind of questions?" she asked.

"About your sister's social life."

Oh. He was talking about the case. That was all right, then. She relaxed a little—but not all that much. "I've already put together a file addressing that." She took it from the pile and placed it on his desk.

"Of course you did," Logan said more to himself than to her.

This woman didn't need his help to be detached, he thought. She needed his help in staying in contact with her human side. And while he was at it, he needed to get her to relax a little. He could *feel* her tension.

"I'm not much on reading," he finally told her after a beat. For now, he ignored the file she'd pushed toward him, preferring the personal touch. "Why don't you just tell me what you wrote, and I'll listen?"

"You're not much on reading," she repeated in disbelief.

If he noticed her reaction, he gave no indication. Instead, he merely shook his head in response. "Not really."

She stared at him. "You're serious?"

"Why?" he asked her innocently, doing an excellent job of hiding his amusement. It was his way of trying to get her to loosen up. In his experience, this was the only way to work a case without letting it get to you. Because if you allowed cases to get to you, it was only a matter of time before they became your undoing, and then you weren't good to anyone, least of all yourself. "Don't I look like I'm serious?"

What he looked like was a guy who didn't have a care in the world—except where his next romantic interlude was coming from.

She wondered if she could appeal to Sean and ask him if anyone else could work on the investigation with her. But then she remembered that technically, she wasn't really supposed to be working on this at all and the investigation belonged to this laid-back detective who seemed more interested in wordplay than in solving six homicides.

She pressed her lips together. Logan Cavanaugh *had* to be better than she thought he was. Otherwise, last name or not, he would be out on his butt. According to what she knew about Brian Cavanaugh, he was a good man who was always there for his men and he didn't suffer idiots. So this all just had to be an act on Logan's part.

Why?

With a sigh, Destiny resigned herself to the fact that it was either work with Logan or return to the bleachers and watch the investigation into her sister's death unfold from the sidelines.

There was absolutely no way she was about to do that. So, for better or worse, she was stuck with the man.

"My mistake," she murmured. "You look serious." And with that, she launched into a summary of what she had entered into the file he wasn't opening.

Chapter 7

There was one thing wrong with the summation that Destiny had given him regarding her sister's social life. For the most part, it involved the past. The present was covered only in generalities. There was no mention of actual names. Was that because there were too many— or because she didn't know any?

"Do you know the names of any of your sister's current friends?" he asked, cutting in when she paused for a breath.

Destiny flushed. "I used to."

God but she hated admitting that.

Once upon a time she and Paula had been closer than two shadows on the wall. But then things began to change. Maybe Paula had seen her as too much of a mother figure and not enough as a sister-confidante. That had come about because she'd been the one left in charge, despite the fact that she wasn't really *that* much older than Paula. It happened out of necessity. Because their father had just walked out on them one day, their mother was forced to take any work she could to pay the bills and hold body and soul together. Most of the time, that took two jobs. Their mother was hardly ever home, which put the burden of responsibility on Destiny's shoulders. Paula grew to resent having to listen to her sister. Rebellion followed.

All in all, though, Paula had turned out all right. She'd gone to college, gotten a degree and went on to make a good career for herself.

And they were finally getting closer again—until this had happened.

"Our careers took us in different directions," she told him. "We moved around in different circles. But we were getting in touch more often again," she said with emphasis.

That wasn't the part he was interested in. "What kind of circles did your sister move around in?" he asked.

Her sister was a fundraiser, working for a charitable foundation. That put her in touch with a broad spectrum of people. Interesting people, Destiny imagined.

"Mainly they had to do with her job."

"Remind me what that was again," he said.

She'd mentioned it in passing in her summary and for a couple of minutes there, he'd been so busy just *watching* Destiny speak that he had lost the thread of what she was saying. That was probably when she'd mentioned her sister's job title.

"She was a fundraiser for the Children's Hospital of

Aurora," Destiny told him again. Was he trying to trip her up? Bait her? Or what? "And she was very good at it. Even in these rough times, she knew just how to coax major corporations and wealthy CEOs into making sizable donations to the hospital."

She knew that because other people had told her. Paula had never been one to sing her own praises, and she didn't talk all that much about work whenever they did get together. Considering all that grief they'd gone through in the middle years, Paula had turned out well and she was proud of her.

Damn it, this shouldn't have happened to you, Paula.

Keeping an angry wave of tears at bay, she said, "The hospital is breaking ground on an oncology wing, thanks to her efforts."

Logan saw the way she was struggling to keep herself under control. To keep the grief at arm's length. He couldn't help but feel sorry for her. But he knew that saying so would be the last thing that she would want to hear. Instead, he said the only thing he knew would be welcome.

"Your sister sounds like she was a really good person."

His remark surprised her. She felt a little salvo of pleasure spread from her stomach and radiate outward. A small smile curved her mouth.

"She was," she acknowledged. "Just not an overly talkative one. At least, not to me." Which really hurt because there'd been a time when they had shared *everything.* "I got the feeling she didn't think I'd understand about the relationship she was hiding from me.

Even when things got better between us, Paula would say that I was too straitlaced."

"Maybe she didn't want to tell you because the guy might have been married." He studied her face to see her reaction to the suggestion.

Defensive of her sister, she began to deny the assumption.

"Paula wouldn't have—" But then Destiny abruptly stopped her own protest. "Well, maybe she did," she amended ruefully. She shook her head. "That would explain why she'd gotten so secretive."

Damn it, Paula, married or not, you should have come to me anyway. Maybe that would have saved your life.

Logan nodded. It was beginning to make more sense. At least they had an avenue to explore. "Considering that she met a lot of powerful men in her line of work, we need to get a list of the hospital's top donors."

That, she knew, would go over like the proverbial lead balloon with Paula's supervisor. "Looking for a killer in that group'll certainly put a crimp into the hospital obtaining any more charitable donations," Destiny prophesized.

"Not if we handle it diplomatically," he replied. He saw the skeptical expression that came over the woman's face. "What? You don't think I can be diplomatic?" He guessed at what she was thinking. "Well, you're wrong. I can be very diplomatic if the situation calls for it," he assured her.

Destiny couldn't picture the man sitting across from

her monitoring every word he uttered. He just didn't seem the type.

"If you say so," she murmured.

"I do." And with that, he rose to his feet. The next moment, Logan was heading toward the door. Destiny had no choice but to move fast if she wanted to catch up to him and not be left behind. "Decided to come along?" he asked innocently.

Destiny shot him a dirty look, but she kept quiet. She felt it was better that way. For both of them.

"Terrible, terrible thing," Marcia Ruben lamented, shaking her head. A crumpled, damp handkerchief was balled up in one of her hands and she dabbed at her eyes periodically as tears insisted on sliding down the highly polished cheeks. Paula's supervisor looked more than a little upset by the news of her death. Paula, she'd already stated twice, had been her very best mover and shaker.

"I don't know what I'm going to do without her. She will be greatly missed by everyone." She took another pass at her cheeks with her handkerchief. "She was the best fundraiser I ever had, and I've been here for a long time," she said with a touch of melancholy. Whether it was for the dead woman or the fact that she had been here for years was anyone's guess. "If there was any way to get another dime out of someone, Paula was the one to do it. Donations just doubled in the short time she worked at the hospital. Given a chance, I'm sure she would have eventually raised enough money to double the size of the hospital. She truly had a gift. It seemed like once Paula got rolling, no one could say no to her."

"Someone obviously had." Destiny wasn't aware that she had said the bitter comment out loud until she heard it herself.

Mrs. Ruben pressed her lips together sadly. "Yes, of course," the heavyset woman readily agreed. "But for the life of me, I cannot begin to imagine how someone could have done that to Paula. Or why."

After telling the woman that Paula was found dead, Destiny had deliberately added that it was staged to look like a suicide. She'd said it to see the expression on Mrs. Ruben's face. There was only horror and disbelief. Either the woman was a very good actress, or she was on the level. Destiny leaned toward the latter.

Pulling herself together, Mrs. Ruben looked from one to the other. "How is it I can help you?"

"We'd like to see a list of the people she approached for donations," Logan told her politely but without any fanfare.

Nonetheless, the woman's small brown eyes widened in stunned disbelief.

"You think that one of them had something to do with Paula's murder? That's impossible," she protested with feeling. "These are people who move around in upper-class circles, who give to the less fortunate—"

She sounded as if she was winding herself up for a long speech. Destiny was quick to head her off.

"We're just trying to follow up every possible avenue, Mrs. Ruben, in the hopes of stumbling onto something that might give us a clue to her killer's identity." She watched the woman's face closely as she added, "We believe that Paula knew her killer."

"How can you be sure?" Mrs. Ruben asked, bewildered.

"There was no sign of a struggle," Logan explained. "Nothing was tossed around. There were no scratches on the vic—on Paula. And no signs of any skin under her nails. She didn't get a chance to fight whoever did this to her. That's because this man caught her off guard."

The woman still appeared rather skeptical. "At the same time, I don't want to insult any of these donors."

"We won't tell them that the list came from you," Logan promised with a sensual smile that seemed to melt the older woman's heart, not to mention her knees.

"Think of it as doing something for Paula," Destiny urged, feeling as if she was moving in for the kill after Logan had softened the woman up.

Mrs. Ruben nodded vigorously. "Yes, of course. For Paula." She wiped away more tears as she turned toward the computer on her desk. "I believe I have the latest list right here. Ah, yes, here it is."

Pulling it up on her screen, the woman hit the print key on her keyboard. The grinding, somewhat labored sound of a machine coming to life was immediately heard from across the aisle. The old printer noisily spit out three pages of names, as well as the companies they were associated with and addresses to go with them.

Since she was the one standing closest to the printer, Destiny gathered together the pages and brought them over to Logan.

"Twenty-six names," she said, looking at Mrs. Ruben.

"Are these all the people she contacted in the last six months?"

"Yes." She bobbed her head up and down, her short, straight hair moving back and forth against her jawline. "Please, tread lightly with these people," she begged. "I don't want them taking offense and withdrawing their pledges." Her voice lowered after a moment's hesitation and the woman said, "I'm afraid they can be very thin-skinned."

"As far as they'll be concerned," Logan told her, "we'll just be asking them if they thought that Paula seemed preoccupied lately, or if she behaved as if something was wrong."

Mrs. Ruben sighed and shook her head. "They'll probably say no. I know that I never saw her looking happier than these last few weeks. She looked as if she was harboring sunbeams."

That, Destiny thought, was the perfect way to describe the Paula she knew and loved. As if she was keeping sunbeams inside of her.

Now it was up to her to find out who put those sunbeams out.

It seemed to Destiny over the course of the next five hours that she was hearing a mantra being repeated over and over again. Every person on the list whom they spoke to expressed shock and dismay at hearing that someone "so young and vital like Paula was murdered." No one could imagine someone doing something so cold-blooded and cruel.

The tall, thin, angular CEO of Practical Engineering, Jacob Deering, asked, "Do you have any suspects in mind?"

"None yet," Logan responded, fielding the question quickly because he was afraid that Destiny might be too honest in her answer.

None of the people they questioned were informed that she was the victim's sister, and he wanted to keep it that way. Nor had they been informed that he and the other investigator thought that Paula's lover might have been responsible for her death.

"Which is why we're going down the list of all the major contributors she dealt with," Logan continued. "Since she spent most of her time around people who could make a difference in building up the hospital's resources, we were hoping that Paula might have said something to you that would send us looking in the right direction for her killer."

The man shook his head. He appeared to be genuinely saddened by the news of her death. "I'm afraid I can't be of any help there. But what I can do is make sure her memory is kept alive by making a personal donation to the hospital in her memory," Deering told them, taking out his checkbook from the center drawer of his desk.

Logan saw the look in Destiny's eyes. She was wondering the same thing he was. Was this donation being made out of a sense of guilt, or was he being honest in wanting to honor Paula's memory?

It was impossible to tell.

Tearing off the check, the CEO of the engineering company who had been high on Paula's list held it out to them. "If you could see that the hospital gets this money—"

"I'm afraid we don't have the actual authority to—" Logan began to demur, but Destiny stepped in and accepted the check.

"We'll be sure to bring it to Mrs. Ruben, her immediate superior," she assured Deering. Then, looking at Logan, she deliberately added, "We did tell Mrs. Ruben that we were going to check in with her late this afternoon."

This was the first he'd heard of it—most likely because she'd just made it up. But for the time being, she was his partner, and that meant backing up her play no matter what. So he did.

"Right. I forgot." Logan kept the charade alive and waited until they were on their way out back to the elevator. "What the hell was that?" he asked once they were alone.

"Well, it's hard to pass up a donation," she told him with a careless shrug. And then her expression turned shrewd. "And this way, we have a sample of his handwriting—in case there's anything in her apartment to match it to." When he looked at her blankly, she spelled it out for him. "Like a love letter."

Logan snorted. Was that it? "Men don't write love letters these days," he pointed out.

"Men like you who don't want to put anything in writing don't write love letters," she readily agreed, getting on the elevator ahead of him. "But an old-fashioned man might."

Where had that come from? "What makes you think

we're looking for an old-fashioned man?" he asked as they rode down.

"I don't, but a lot of these men have held down their positions for a number of years, making them older, and there's no sense in ruling that out yet, is there?" The way she asked, the question was rhetorical. "If we don't know who we're looking for, we have to take all the different options into consideration."

He didn't see anything to argue with. "You have a point," he agreed.

"Yeah, well, I just wish I had an answer," Destiny said, more to herself than to him. The doors opened on the ground floor and she all but charged out. "C'mon," she tossed over her shoulder, "we've still got more names on this list."

For someone who'd slept on her desk last night, she seemed to have an incredible amount of energy, Logan thought darkly as he followed in her wake.

"How about a drink?" he suggested. They'd finally talked to their last donor—with no luck—and it was the tail end of a very long, long day. Evening was flirting with the darkening sky, and he was ready to put down his shield for the night.

But Destiny shook her head in response to his offer. "I don't drink," she told him. "I find that it clouds the mind."

"It also helps unclench your jaw," he told her pointedly.

She instantly squared her shoulders. "My jaw's not clenched," she retorted.

"You don't see it from my vantage point." He held his hands up, knowing she would take offense. "Look, you can't deny that if you were any stiffer, you could double as a landing field. Take a break. Relax. In the morning we'll review our notes and maybe get a fresh perspective on things," he told her. "But that's not going to happen if you don't go home and get some sleep."

Maybe because she'd been left in charge so early in her life, but she had never liked being told what to do, and she balked at it now.

"Don't worry, I'll get some sleep," she told him dismissively.

He wasn't placated. "On a surface that doesn't involve steel or wood," he told her pointedly. And then he smiled a smile that she was certain someone must have told him was boyish and charming—and while it was both those things, she also found it annoying. "I personally recommend dinner, a drink and a hot shower."

"Good, then you can eat, drink and wash," she told him.

"Don't make me get tough, Richardson," he warned. There was a glint in Logan's eyes that she couldn't quite read.

Destiny thought about ignoring him, but she had a feeling that he wasn't going to drop this until he saw her getting up and leaving the precinct.

Okay, if that was the way he wanted to play it, she could do that. She could leave. But she wasn't going to go home. She wanted to go back to her sister's apartment and see what she could find there now that she had something to look for—a love letter or a note, or some sort of communication that could give her more of a hint as to just who had killed her sister.

Or, at the very least, maybe she could discover the identity of the person her sister had been involved with before everything had fallen so ignobly apart.

"Okay. I'll go home," she agreed docilely.

This was too easy. Logan eyed her suspiciously. "Okay?" he echoed. "Just like that?"

"Just like that," she repeated innocently. She smiled at him, doing her best to seem guileless. "You're very persuasive."

He laughed, shaking his head. "And you must think I'm very dumb."

"No, on the contrary," she told him. "I think you're very smart and you make a lot of sense." She looked down at the outfit she'd had on now for close to forty-eight hours. "Besides, I *am* beginning to feel like I smell a little gamey in this outfit," she told him. "I could stand to take a hot shower, maybe eat a sandwich and then get some rest. I feel dead on my feet," she confessed with just the right note of sincerity to sell this.

Logan's expression was impassive as he appraised her. For just a moment, his mind had conjured up the image of her naked, with the hot water hitting her body. It took him a long moment to tear his mind away. When he did, he nodded at what she'd just said. "Nice to hear you being reasonable."

She shot him a wide smile. "Maybe you're just rubbing off on me."

"I'll walk you to your car," he told her once they'd reached the ground floor.

"Not necessary," Destiny protested, but only marginally since she knew he expected it. If she made too much of a big deal about his walking her to her car, he might suspect that she wasn't going home the way she'd told him.

"Humor me," he said.

"You're the primary on this," she responded, symbolically waving a white flag.

So he walked her to her car, and under his watchful eye she got in behind the steering wheel and turned her ignition key. The car was instantly ready to peel out. Instead, she slowly eased out of her parking spot.

Using her rearview mirror, she could still see Logan watching her as she pulled out of the parking lot.

Destiny didn't let go of the breath she was holding until she had gone more than a mile. Remaining vigilant, she saw no sign of his vehicle following hers.

She'd made good her escape.

Releasing a deep, cleansing breath, she turned her car toward Paula's apartment.

Chapter 8

The yellow police tape was still up. Just as she'd hoped, the police guard was gone.

Destiny tried not to focus on the tape as she ducked under it. Just seeing it there, before the door of the apartment where Paula had lived, created an eerie, oppressive sensation in the middle of her chest.

Using her key, Destiny let herself into the apartment, then eased the door closed behind her.

Only then did she reach for the light switch and turn it on. The moment she did, she jumped, startled. Her gun was in her hand in less than a heartbeat despite the fact that her heart was beating fast enough to break the sound barrier.

"Easy, it's just me," Logan said to her, his hands up as he took a couple of steps toward her. And then, he slowly dropped them to his sides, watching her with awe. "My God, that's the fastest I've ever seen anyone draw their weapon. You should enter some sort of competition. You'd win, hands down—no pun intended," he tacked on.

Destiny drew in a deep breath, trying to steady her nerves. For a split second, she'd thought she'd stumbled across her sister's killer.

"What the *hell* are you doing here?" she demanded, holstering her weapon. It took all she could do to keep her hands from shaking.

"Same thing as you," Logan answered mildly. Actually, that wasn't true. He was here to see what she'd look for, fairly certain that left on her own, she wasn't all that keen about sharing what she found.

"I could have shot you," she cried. Didn't he realize that? Why had he been there, in the dark like some kind of creature of the night?

"But you didn't," Logan countered. "I like to look on the bright side," he added.

"How did you know I'd come here?" she asked. There was no other way to interpret his standing there in the dark like that. He'd been lying in wait for her, confident that she was going to show up, even though she'd told him she was going home.

"Just a hunch." Because she was obviously waiting for more, he elaborated. "You had me going for a while—until you said that I was the primary."

"Well, you are," she said. It came out almost like an accusation.

"It was more the way you said it," he amended. Logan shook his head. "It came out much too docile for you."

"What are you, an expert on me now?" Destiny stared at him, completely mystified. "You've only known me for, what, a day?"

"Almost two," he corrected, as if that explained it all. "And sometimes, you just know things." He smiled at her with an air of satisfaction that immediately got under her skin. "I would have done the same in your shoes."

Her eyes narrowed as she tried to understand. Was he drawing parallels between them? Or was he just trying to get her to drop her guard?

Don't hold your breath, Cavanaugh.

"So exactly what are you saying? That I'm just like you?"

"Oh, God, I hope not." He said it with such feeling that just for a split second, she believed him. "What fun would that be?"

Was that how he viewed his job? This investigation? As fun? Was he *that* irreverent?

"I wasn't aware that we were supposed to be having fun," she said cynically.

"You create little pockets of it along the way," he told her, and she had the feeling that despite the easygoing smile on his lips, Logan was absolutely serious. "Otherwise, this job'll eat you alive."

For now, she let that go. "How did you get here ahead of me?" she asked. "I drove away with you still standing in the parking lot, watching me leave."

"I took a shortcut," he told her. "Besides, I have the car with the pretty little dancing lights and the siren I can turn on whenever I'm stuck in traffic."

"What would you have done if I hadn't come here?" she challenged.

"Oh, but you did, and I figured it was a pretty safe bet from where I was standing. So," he said, getting down to business, "what is it that we're going to be looking for?"

For a second, the private part, the part that had always been protective of Paula and their mother before that, wanted to defiantly dig in. But what was the point? Protecting Paula no longer really mattered. What mattered was not letting whoever had done this to her sister get away with it. And if that person was the serial killer the way she believed him to be, well, then finding him and making him pay for all this as well as keeping him from killing anyone else would at least in some minor way give some sort of meaning to Paula's death.

She shrugged her shoulders in answer to his question. "Something. Anything."

"Well, that's really pinning it down." He laughed shortly. "In other words, we'll 'know' it when we see it."

"Yes." And then, as he began to head toward Paula's bedroom to conduct a second, more thorough search through her closet and bureau drawers, Destiny recalled something. She addressed his back. "When we were kids, Paula used to keep a diary. I don't know if she still does—still did," Destiny corrected herself, still struggling with the fact that she had to use the past tense. "But it's worth looking for."

The first wave of crime scene investigators had taken the laptop they'd found—presumably Paula's—back to the precinct. The technician who had gone over it—

Brenda Cavanaugh—the chief of D's daughter-in-law—was exceptionally thorough.

"They didn't find anything besides her daily schedule on her computer," Logan told her.

That was no surprise. "They wouldn't have," Destiny told him, beginning her search in the kitchen. "In some ways, Paula was kind of old-fashioned. She liked the thought of writing personal things down using a pen and paper." Her mouth curved just a little as she remembered her sister's words. "Paula said she thought it was more 'romantic' that way."

Logan paused and glanced in her direction. "Sounds like she was a really unique person."

Destiny suppressed the heartfelt sigh that rose in her throat.

God, but she was going to miss Paula. Even though they hadn't gotten together all that much and Paula had her own set of friends, friends that she gathered she, Destiny, didn't have all that much in common with, she would miss the *idea* of Paula, the comforting feeling that Paula was somewhere in the world with her. Now she had to accept the cold, hard fact that she would never see Paula again no matter how much she wanted it or how hard she wished for it.

Her baby sister was gone, and she couldn't do anything about it.

But the next best thing would be finding Paula's killer and making him pay for this. It was all she had to cling to.

"Yeah, she was," Destiny agreed in a small, strained voice.

With that, she turned back to the kitchen and began opening all the drawers, checking all the shelves, including the refrigerator and the freezer. Paula wouldn't have put it somewhere obvious, not since Destiny had accidentally stumbled across it under her sister's mattress when she was changing the sheets years ago. Because Paula had become secretive and uncommunicative, she'd read a couple of pages—just enough to discover that David Chesnee had been Paula's first and that Paula had been disappointed because there were no shooting stars, no wild feelings of fulfillment.

That was as far as she'd gotten before Paula walked in and caught her. Absolutely livid, Paula didn't talk to her for a month.

With all her heart, she wished that Paula wasn't talking to her now. That it was just anger and not death that separated them.

Pressing her lips together, she blinked several times to keep back the tears. She had no time for tears.

Destiny moved about the kitchen methodically, carefully going through one section at a time. But the result was still the same. She was coming up empty. The diary—if it existed—wasn't wrapped in a plastic bag and tucked in the recesses of the refrigerator. It wasn't in a plastic case on the bottom of the freezer. And it definitely wasn't in any of the cabinets or the small pantry.

Stumped, Destiny was on the verge of admitting that her sister no longer kept something as old-fashioned as a diary when her foot hit the bottom of the refrigerator. The long, rectangular plastic section just beneath the refrigerator door came loose.

She looked down at it and frowned. She had the same problem with the one in her apartment. Having removed it to clean the coils in the front, she'd found that reattaching the section was far trickier than she had anticipated. It kept coming loose, bedeviling her. In Paula's case, Destiny doubted that she'd taken it off to clean the coils. Cleaning had never exactly been high on her sister's priority list. Most likely she—

Destiny stopped and stared at the loose section as if seeing it for the first time.

The next moment, she dropped to her knees in front of the refrigerator. Pushing the rectangular section out of the way, Destiny reached beneath the refrigerator as far as she could. Fingers outstretched, she felt around.

Which was just the way Logan found her, hunkered down, flat on the floor with her arm underneath the refrigerator. Not knowing what to think, only that she was lying on the floor, he rushed over to her. Logan quickly got down on the floor beside her.

"Richardson, you okay?" he asked, concerned.

She could have sworn that her fingertips had just barely brushed against something. Positive it had to be the diary, she focused on coaxing it out and was oblivious to whatever Cavanaugh was saying.

The next moment, a pair of strong hands pulled her back, away from the refrigerator. And then, just as if she was some weightless rag doll, she was off the floor and in his arms. How she'd gotten turned around, she wasn't sure. Just as she wasn't sure how he'd managed to get her up without tearing off the arm that had been snaked under the refrigerator. The only thing she *did* know was that there were less than two inches between them and she found herself looking into those magnetic green eyes of his.

Her stomach tightened into a knot. He was much too close.

There was concern written all over his face. "What happened?" he asked. Then, before she had a chance to utter a single word, Logan urgently demanded, "Are you all right?"

For just a split second, as her breath struggled to move back into her lungs, Destiny was utterly at a loss for words. Her mind had gone numb. But not her body. Her body felt as if a blanket of heat was wrapped all around her.

And then, with a determined surge of strength, she pulled herself together. The heat receded and her senses returned. Her mind was functioning again.

"Yeah, I'm fine, except that I think my right arm is longer than my left one now." The sarcastic tone faded as she told him, "I think I felt something." Turning, she pointed to the refrigerator. "It's under there. I'm sure of it."

"It's probably just dust—or the dead carcass of a rodent," he guessed.

She blocked the latter image from her mind. She'd seen more than her share of dead bodies—Paula's included—but a dead rat made her squeamish.

"No," she insisted, "this felt like something straight and flat—like the edge of one of those black-and-white copybooks. You know the kind I'm talking about." She looked at him expectantly, as if, for this one moment, he could access her thoughts.

A black-and-white copybook could have easily been turned into a diary, he thought. At any rate, since she seemed so positive, it was worth a look.

"Stand back," he told her. "If it's there, I'll get it out."

Destiny shook her head. "Your arm's too big to angle under the refrigerator," she told him. "You'll only get stuck."

He was way ahead of her there. "Wasn't planning to go under it," he said.

And then, very slowly, grasping the side of the refrigerator closest to him, he moved it as far as he could. Positioning himself on the other side of the appliance, he repeated the process. Logan went back and forth several times until he'd finally succeeded in "walking" the refrigerator away from the wall and out into the kitchen proper.

It was all the encouragement Destiny needed. Hopping onto the counter, Destiny slid her bottom along the slick tile. Perched on the edge, she looked down into the space he'd created.

She could see a corner of a black-and-white book. Triumph surged through her. "I was right. It's a copybook."

He looked around the refrigerator he'd just taken for a dance. "She really had trust issues, didn't she?" he marveled.

Now, there was an ironic observation, given that they were about to read her sister's most intimate, personal thoughts.

"Obviously justified," Destiny retorted defensively for the sister who could no longer defend herself.

Scrambling over to one side, Destiny lowered herself into the small space. There wasn't really much room between the appliance and the wall. She had just enough space to bend her knees. Sinking down as far as she could go, Destiny once more felt around.

Tapping into her patience—it was more difficult than she'd anticipated—Destiny finally managed to secure the book using just the edge of her fingertips. She moved it closer and closer to her until she could finally wrap her fingers around one corner.

She didn't like what she was feeling.

The book was wet, as if the refrigerator had just recently leaked on it—or it had been dropped into something wet before someone slipped it back beneath the refrigerator.

But if that was the case, why go through all that trouble if she was dead?

Unless she hadn't been dead at the time.

But then, if there was something in the diary someone else didn't want coming to light, why not just take the diary and destroy it?

It didn't make sense.

Still, there might be some clue they could get off one of the pages. With a less than triumphant sigh, she placed the rippled copybook on the counter next to her point of entry.

Seeing what he assumed was the diary, Logan marveled, "Son of a gun, you're right."

Trying to vault out of the enclosure, to her dismay

Destiny discovered that her upper-body strength was not as good as she would have liked. Two more attempts to propel herself out of the small space failed before she finally turned her eyes toward Logan.

Logan appeared to be entertained by her unsuccessful attempts to get out of the small, enclosed area. His smile was annoying and far sexier than she would have been willing to admit.

"Can I get you something?" he offered. "A ladder maybe?" The suggestion was followed by the sound of his laughter.

Ordinarily, Destiny might have enjoyed the deep, somewhat sensual rumbling sound. But right now, she just felt exasperated.

"Okay, a little help here." It was just short of a demand.

"Sure thing," he said obligingly. "All you had to do was just ask."

"Otherwise you'd just stand there for the rest of the night?" she asked.

He looked at her as if she'd gone simpleminded. "And get my head bitten off? Nope. I find that with women, to stay on the safe side, you have to wait until they make a request. *Then* you can come riding to the rescue."

"Let's get this clear. This is *not* riding to my rescue," she informed him.

"It's not?" Logan said innocently. "Then what is it?"

"This is just giving me a helping hand," she fired back through gritted teeth.

He gave the impression of weighing her words. Finally, Logan lifted his shoulders in a careless shrug and said, "Whatever you say."

He was still laughing at her, even though there wasn't a sound. Losing patience, she said, "Get me out of here, Cavanaugh!"

"Your wish is my command," he assured her.

The next moment, he put his hands on each side of her rib cage. With what seemed to be a minimum of effort, Logan easily lifted her out of the narrow space behind the refrigerator.

Bringing her up and over the counter, his hands slipped a fraction of an inch and he wound up holding her along the sides of her breasts.

If that wasn't bad enough, somehow, as he brought her over the top, she'd wound up being *much* too close to Logan. For all intents and purposes, she was almost intimately close.

In response, her heart had begun hammering again and then that damn breath of hers had all but disappeared for a second time. But this time, exertion had nothing to do with it.

Proximity did.

When Logan set her down, the counter was against her back and he was pretty much against her front—or so it felt to her.

The world seemed to suddenly freeze in time for a moment—except that there was no ice, just heat. Lots and lots of heat, and it flashed back and forth between them with an intensity that would have taken her breath away—had she had any to take.

What the hell was going on with her? The question

came on the heels of her reaction. Her *atypical* reaction. For a second—for just the briefest of seconds—she felt a very real, very strong temptation—to kiss Logan.

His lips were less than the breadth of an eyelash away from hers. All she had to do was rise up on her toes, tilt her face up to his and there they were.

The temptation was enormous.

Especially when she felt Logan's breath along her face. The ache inside of her, hot and strong, came out of nowhere.

Destiny tried to tell herself that it came out of the emptiness she was experiencing because of Paula's death, but that still didn't make it go away or even lessen its intensity by so much as a fraction.

The longing grew.

Her pulse began to race as the urge multiplied, growing by leaps and bounds until it all but threatened to swallow her up.

What would be the harm? her conscience whispered, turning on her. *What would be the harm, just this once, to give in?*

Chapter 9

Damn, but he was tempted. *Really, really* tempted.

If they weren't working together, if they weren't focused on trying to find who had killed her sister and possibly several other women, Logan would have felt freer to indulge his curiosity.

But he *was* walking a tightrope here.

It was up to him to make perfectly sure there were no missteps with this investigation so that if they actually found a viable suspect, the case wouldn't be tossed out of court on some irritating-as-hell technicality.

Like tainted evidence.

Would kissing a fellow investigator in an unplanned moment of extreme attraction and overwhelming weakness be considered the basis for undermining such an investigation? Logan would have been the first to admit that he wasn't really clear on the concept, but all the same, he didn't think so.

Or was it that he didn't *want* it to be so?

Oh, the hell with it, he thought with a surge of impatience as he symbolically threw up his hands in frustration.

The next moment those hands framed her face—odd how delicate she actually felt, considering that she came on like some indestructible gangbuster.

And then, anticipation coursing through his veins, Logan lowered his head and contact was made.

Extremely pleasant contact.

No, on second thought, Logan amended, the word *pleasant* had no place here. Mainly because the kiss wasn't *pleasant*. It was overwhelming, breath stealing, earthmoving and a whole host of other descriptions meant to convey something incredible, something *leagues* out of the ordinary. *Pleasant* was a word meant to describe an old-fashioned drawing room comedy or a semicold beer—rather than a preferable completely cold one. *Pleasant* was a joke that made you smile, not laugh out loud.

This kiss made him want to *shout*.

Logan could almost *feel* his blood rushing through his veins and definitely could feel his adrenaline increasing in tempo. As for his heart, it was hammering so hard, he was surprised it hadn't broken through his rib cage and fallen at her feet.

Without fully meaning to, he deepened the kiss, and lost himself in the revelry.

Oh, no, no, no!

What was she doing? Destiny silently demanded. Why was she kissing him back? She should be the one calling a halt to this, the one setting an example, not melting in his arms.

But the plain truth of it was, despite the fact that she knew all the reasons she shouldn't be doing this, she knew of only one reason why she should.

Because she wanted it to continue.

Wanted to just lose herself in this man with the lethal lips. Wanted, just for a moment, not to think about *anything*. Not death, not being alone.

Not even Paula.

For this sliver of a moment in time she wanted just to *feel*. To absorb hot sensations and not make excuses or place them into neatly labeled categories.

Was that so wrong?

Yes, when it interferes with getting your job done. When it interferes with getting Paula's killer.

She had a dozen arguments against what was happening. And only one for it. It made her feel human. More than that, it made her *feel* something, and she hadn't been in that particular place in her life for a very long while now. Long before she had discovered Paula's lifeless body in the tub.

The desire that sprang up within her was fierce, intense, and it took her by surprise as it barreled through her.

Stop! Destiny ordered herself. There was too much for her to do to dally like this, to allow this sort of thing to happen.

And yet…

Oh, and yet this was so delicious....

With effort steeped in the strict discipline that had seen her through so many difficult phases of her life, Destiny finally managed to pull her head back.

For a moment, they were both silent, looking at one another, trying to gauge the other's thoughts and finding that they couldn't.

Right now, Destiny secretly admitted that she was having trouble gauging her own thoughts, much less his. And more than anything, she really wished her damn pulse would stop racing like that. It made her dizzy and breathless.

But then, so did he, she realized.

Get a grip. This isn't the time or the place!

"I think we'd better take a look at this copybook before we bag and tag it," she heard herself say to Logan as she awkwardly dropped her hands to her sides. Her voice, sounding hoarse to begin with, cracked by the time she came to the end of her statement.

Her eyes on his, she held her breath. She hadn't the slightest idea if he would pick up her cue—or demand to know if she was trying to lead him on and play him for a fool for some reason.

It seemed like an eternity later before Logan finally nodded.

"Makes sense," he agreed.

Only then did she realize that Logan was still holding her by the shoulders. The next moment, he released her.

Once that last contact was broken, Destiny suddenly felt unsteady—and alone again.

Taking a breath, she nodded at the refrigerator, stand-

ing now like a lone sentry in the middle of the tiny
kitchen.

"We'd better push that back where it was. Otherwise,
it might look suspicious. We're not supposed to be here,"
she reminded him in case he didn't understand why
she wanted the appliance moved back against the wall.

It was the added explanation that brought a grin
to his lips. "You just figured that out now?" he asked
glibly.

Destiny resisted getting sucked into another round
of trading remarks, even though for some reason the
thought seemed oddly comforting to her. Maybe because that made it business as usual, or at least what
seemed to be passing as usual between them.

Right now, she thought, looking down at the copybook, they might be holding the key to everything in
their hands. Mentally, she crossed her fingers.

But the second she opened the copybook, Destiny
felt her heart sink.

Despite the fact that it was definitely written in Paula's hand, the pages between the covers were warped
and the ink was all but washed out thanks to the leak
from the refrigerator. Water had penetrated the thicker
cover and had gotten through to most of the pages,
making them semi or completely illegible, depending
on what section she turned to.

Nonetheless, she placed the copybook on the counter and carefully turned each page, doing her best not
to let them shred beneath her fingertips.

Disappointed, Logan shook his head as he looked at

the halos of blue ink that seemed to brand each page to a greater or lesser degree.

"You're not going to get anything out of that," he told her. "You're just wasting your time."

Determined to find one viable scrap of *something*, Destiny was not about to give up.

"My time to waste," she said defiantly. "You're free to go home at any time, you know. You don't have to stay here waiting for me to get finished."

"I'm primary," he reminded her. "That means I'm responsible for you while we're working the case." He didn't add that he'd been told to keep an eye on her during the investigation. It didn't take a genius to know she would take offense at that.

"Not if you didn't know I was here," she pointed out. And if he hadn't played a hunch and shown up at the apartment, he *wouldn't* have known she was here.

His smile was amused—and damn annoying—as he said, "But I do."

Destiny sighed. Arguing with this man was like willingly banging her head against a wall—and just about as satisfying. Deciding to ignore him, she went back to carefully scanning each and every page.

She'd almost gone through the whole thin book when she saw it. A section that hadn't absorbed water from the leaking refrigerator.

And there was writing on it.

Every inch of her became alert as she squinted at the dry pages. There were still words missing, words that probably had gotten a little wet and then faded away when the paper dried. But she could make out a name. Just barely.

Her eyes widened. "Drake Simmons."

Because watching her turn pages threatened to put him to sleep, Logan had begun a second survey throughout the kitchen, going through spice jars at random, looking beneath the sink. The sound of her hushed voice had him looking up.

"What did you say?"

Beckoning him over, she waited until he was beside her and then she pointed to the top of the page that had caught her attention. She ran the tip of her finger beneath a line. "It looks like she wrote down 'Drake Simmons.'"

For a second, he couldn't recall where he'd seen the name before. And then it came to him. That was the last name on the list of contributors that Mrs. Ruben had given them.

Glancing over Destiny's shoulder at the copybook on the counter, he could make out the name—now that she'd said it. But nothing else, either before the name or after it, was even remotely clear.

Logan raised his eyes to hers. His were far less exhilarated than hers.

"Is she just mentioning that she has an appointment to see him, or did she make this notation because they had a date?" he asked.

Destiny shook her head. "I can't make out anything that would tell us," she said haplessly.

"When she kept a diary, was it just to chronicle who

she had a crush on, or was it like a miniautobiography?" he asked her.

Destiny wished with all her heart it was the former but she had to be honest.

"More like the latter. Paula liked rereading sections of it to see where her head was at at a particular time. I got the impression that her diary wasn't just to record the way she felt about things—or any one person. It was the sum total of her day-to-day activities."

"Great," he muttered. Then, curious, he asked, "Did you keep a diary like your sister?"

She shook her head. "I was too busy—and much too tired at the end of the day to come up with the energy to write. Why?" she asked.

Logan lifted his shoulders in a careless shrug, turning into the personification of innocence right in front of her eyes.

"No reason," he assured her. "Just curious."

Her gut told her that there was more to it than that, but it was safer all around not to push the subject. Maybe if she didn't, it would fade away.

Just like the effects of his kiss.

Yeah, good luck with that, she mocked herself. Because right now, she could still feel his lips on hers, and it was doing one hell of a number on the rest of her.

Destiny made a mental note not to let it happen again.

Having gleaned every single shred of information possible from her sister's body, the medical examiner released Paula's remains to her the next day. The doctor, a grandfatherly type who looked as if he was more suited to donning a Santa Claus costume and gathering small children onto his knee than meticulously dissecting bodies and then sewing them together again, looked at Destiny with kindness in his eyes. He was accustomed to working with her looking over his shoulder and asking questions, not having her as the deceased's next of kin. It made for a very awkward, uncomfortable situation.

"I'm really very, very sorry for your loss, Destiny," Raymond Mathews said in a low, sympathetic voice, his Deep South upbringing weaving itself around every syllable. "Doesn't seem like nearly enough to say, but I am."

She did her best to smile as she nodded her head. "Thank you," she murmured.

This was such an unnatural position for her to be in. She was ordinarily on the clinical end of things, not the emotional end. She felt guilty and angry and incredibly sad as she viewed her sister's reconstructed body.

The stitching, she noted, was exceptionally neat and small. Dr. Matthews had taken extra care to try to call as little attention as possible to the fact that her sister had been autopsied, and she appreciated it. Appreciated, too, though she had no idea how to express it, that rather than continue the investigation on his own while she was busy, Logan seemed to have opted to accompany her down to the M.E.'s terrain to reclaim her sister.

Logan watched her now, for the moment fading into the shadows. He'd sensed, despite her claims to the contrary and insisting that she was "fine," that Destiny could really use someone to lean on.

He was also fairly certain that his father's chief assistant was far too stubborn to admit as much. His suspicions were validated when, after telling him that he didn't need to do this, he saw a flicker of gratitude in her sky-blue eyes.

Which was why he also "tagged along," a silent but strong presence, when she went to make final arrangements at the funeral home.

Edward Michaels, the director of Michaels & Sons, the funeral home that Sean had referred her to, appeared momentarily surprised when she said that she didn't want the typical three-day viewing period for her sister.

"I want the funeral to take place tomorrow, so just do what you have to do to get my sister ready," she told the man.

"Why are you in such a hurry?" Logan commented in a low voice, meant only for her ears.

"I'm not," she bit off impatiently, then reined in her temper.

This wasn't Logan's fault. It wasn't anyone's fault—except for whoever had done this to Paula. She had to remember to keep her anger focused in the right direction and not let it flare the way it had been these past few days. She couldn't allow her normally even temper to be all over the map like this.

She lifted her shoulders in an indifferent shrug, letting them drop again. "She's dead. I don't want people staring at her."

Destiny couldn't remember the last time she'd felt so drained. Maybe never. The moment the medical examiner had released Paula's body to be transported, she'd gotten on the phone and called every number Paula had listed in her cell phone. She informed each and every one of the more than one hundred people of Paula's death, listened to their words of shock and condolences, then quietly told each person on the other end of her phone where and when the funeral services would be held.

Exhausted, she'd gone directly to the funeral home from there. Her shadow had insisted on accompanying her despite her protests. She was secretly grateful he had. She wasn't all that sure she was up to driving back to the precinct again.

And then, out of the blue, she thought of something.

Logan saw the startled expression on her face and automatically turned around. He expected to see someone walking into the chapel-quiet room.

But there was no one in it but the two of them. The director was still there, but he was just about to slip out of the room.

"What's the matter?" Logan asked her.

"I just realized that I'm going to have to hold a reception for the people who attend the funeral, aren't I? They're going to want to eat afterward." She closed her eyes, as if searching for strength. She wasn't given to hosting even intimate get-togethers over dinner, much less something on such a large scale.

Logan smiled. He might not be able to help her deal with the pain, but here at least he could provide her with the kind of help she needed.

"Don't worry," he assured her. "I can handle the reception for you."

Destiny looked at him, slightly bewildered. What was he saying? That he'd direct all the attending mourners to the local fast-food/take-out restaurant for her?

"You?" she echoed, waiting for him to explain further.

"Well, not me directly," he qualified with a laugh. Boiling eggs was a challenge for him. But it was all about networking and knowing where to turn. "But I can get this covered for you," he promised.

This new, enlarged family of his was turning out to be very handy. All he had to do in this case was call Andrew Cavanaugh. He was fairly certain he didn't even have to give the man all the particulars of the situation. The man's abilities to pull meals together—be they for four people or four hundred—were all but legendary.

On top of that, according to what his father told him, the former chief of police thoroughly enjoyed doing it. He'd heard that there was none better when it came to having everything ready at the same time as well as *on* time.

"You're telling me you have access to a fairy godmother?" she quipped. To her, holding a last-minute reception—and pulling it off with some amount of success—was in the realm of magic.

Logan grinned at her. She was beginning to find that grin more and more unsettling—as well as annoyingly appealing.

"Almost."

"With their own cooking show?" she added, because

as far as she was concerned, it would take a professional to pull this off. Everyone she called to tell them about Paula had sincerely promised to be there. Her sister's friends and coworkers were that affected by the news of her death.

"Even better," Logan told her. He paused for dramatic effect, though for the life of him he wouldn't have been able to say why helping her out both amused and pleased him as much as it did. "This is my father's brother's specialty. From what I'm told, you just have to tell him approximately how many people to expect and he'll take it from there."

Though she still found it hard to accept such effortless generosity, it was a tremendous relief.

"I'm not sure," she confessed. "Two hundred, two hundred and fifty." And if they all brought someone with them, that would make the number all but unmanageable.

Who was she kidding? If she were doing this, feeding four people would be unmanageable to her.

But Logan appeared completely unshaken by the fluctuating response. Instead, he merely nodded and said, "Hence the word *approximate*. Don't worry, 'Uncle' Andrew can handle it. The man loves a challenge, and from what I've heard he's never had a single occasion where he's run out of food or had to turn someone away. He's close to a miracle worker," he added without any fanfare.

There was just one small problem. "But he doesn't know me."

"Maybe not, but he knows me and I know you—as

does my dad." His eyes held hers. He could see another protest coming. It was obvious that the woman didn't like to be beholden to anyone. "Let me do this one thing for you," he said softly.

Damn it, there went her pulse again. At the most inopportune time, she thought in unbridled annoyance. What *was* it about Logan Cavanaugh that messed so badly with her inner peace?

"Okay," she heard herself saying. "If you think he won't mind—"

"He won't."

"—I'd really appreciate it," she concluded.

He was on his cell phone, calling his father, before she'd uttered the last word.

Chapter 10

Destiny stood off to the side of the living room, looking around at all the people here and throughout the first floor and the backyard. Earlier, they'd filled the small church beyond its capacity.

She'd had no idea that Paula had touched so many people. Her sister had certainly come a long way from the angry, rebellious teenager who insisted on arguing with her over everything at every turn. Paula had obviously gotten it together far better than she had, Destiny thought with no small pride. God knew she didn't know this many people.

The people she'd called to notify about her sister's funeral service had obviously called other people, and the small church where the service was held had gone from full to standing room only.

There, again, Logan had surprised her by coming

through for her. Although both she and Paula had had religious instructions as children, they'd drifted away from attending Sunday services or being part of any church in Aurora. She knew Paula would have wanted someone officiating over her funeral, and the thought of leaving it up to the funeral director hadn't really been what she'd wanted to do.

"How about my uncle Adam?" Logan had asked her when she'd told him the problem.

"What about your uncle Adam?" she'd said. She hadn't even known Logan *had* an uncle Adam, but that was obviously no longer the question. Why was he volunteering the man?

As it turned out, Father Adam Cavelli belonged to Logan's first family—the relatives he and his siblings had grown up believing were his father's brothers and sisters. Father Adam was a priest at St. Jude, a small, fifty-year-old church located on the far side of Aurora. When the hospital mix-up between his father and the real Sean Cavelli had come to light, the priest had made it clear that he was still their uncle, still loved them just the same as he had when they had been "the bratty Cavellis, driving saints crazy," and nothing would change that. He'd told them that he would continue to be available to them anytime, day or night.

It was when Logan told her that his uncle could take care of her sister's funeral service that she'd stared at her new partner in utter, fascinated disbelief.

"My God, Logan, you Cavanaughs are like one-stop shopping. Police protection, legal counsel, dinner and last rites—it's all taken care of in one neat little package. Unbelievable!"

"You might not want to say 'dinner' and 'last rites' in the same breath if you're talking around Uncle Andrew," Logan had advised. "He might not find it amusing."

Flustered, she'd murmured, "Right." There was no way she wanted to take a chance on insulting Andrew Cavanaugh, even accidentally.

So, thanks to Logan's efforts and, she was certain, in no small way Sean's input, she had both the funeral services and the reception that immediately followed all taken care of. That left her with very little to do—except to grieve.

No, damn it, you don't have time to wallow and indulge yourself, she silently upbraided herself now.

Paula's killer might be somewhere in this crowd of people, paying their last respects. Observing the effects of what he'd done. Getting high on the grief. She couldn't afford to let herself come apart. She couldn't fail Paula now. This was all she could still give Paula—her killer's head on a platter.

Standing next to her, Logan could feel Destiny tensing, and he automatically looked around to see if there was anything wrong. It was a large area to scan. The former chief of police had thrown open his doors—literally—and people drifted in and out, making use of not just the house but the patio and the garden beyond that.

Nothing seemed to stand out to him.

"What's wrong?" he asked Destiny. "Other than the obvious."

She took a deep breath before answering him, still carefully surveying the immediate area. "Her killer might be here."

Logan had his doubts about that. "I really don't think that—"

Impatient, she cut him off. "Think about it. The killer was someone Paula'd had a relationship with. Everyone listed on her cell phone told me they'd be here, and they are. Not only that, but they brought other people who knew Paula. Whoever she was involved with *had* to be on that cell phone list. Which means he's got to be here. I can feel it," she insisted.

Logan reconsidered. He supposed her argument had merit. Looking around again, he found the numbers to be almost overwhelming. If the killer was here, it was a matter of hiding in plain sight.

"So what do you want to do?" he asked Destiny.

Catching killers was a combination of luck and skill, she'd come to decide. Mainly luck.

"Mingle. Talk. Hopefully pick up on something." Right now, there was nothing else they could do.

"In other words, interact with the guests." He didn't see that as being any different from what one would expect a family member in this circumstance to do at a funeral reception. "Okay," he agreed.

Something in Logan's voice caught her attention. He was volunteering to join her. That wasn't what she'd had in mind. "I didn't mean that you had to do this, too."

There was no way she was getting rid of him, Logan

thought. Granted, Destiny was putting up a tough exterior, but he had three sisters. He knew an act when he saw one. Destiny was both fragile and vulnerable inside. She needed him.

"Two sets of ears are better than one," he told her philosophically. "Besides, I'm the—"

"Primary," she concluded for him. "Yes, I know." There was no note of exasperation in her voice the way there had been the other times. "Okay, 'Primary,'" she agreed. "Let's see what we can discover."

What she discovered was that, at least on the surface, Paula apparently had no enemies. Everyone thought the world of her. And, despite the fact that there were several people Paula had considered to be *very* close friends, not one of them had a clue who her new lover had been. Unlike all the other times she was seeing someone, this time she'd become very secretive, and for the most part she seemed exceedingly happy.

Until the night she'd sent out her last text message to her close group of friends.

Destiny felt as if they were going around in circles. It was getting incredibly frustrating for her.

"Why don't you take a break?"

The suggestion came from a deep voice behind her. Turning, she found herself looking up into Andrew Cavanaugh's slightly lined, kindly face. His eyes reminded her of Logan's, she realized.

"A break?" she echoed, not really sure what the former police chief and present-day miracle worker was telling her.

Andrew smiled at her knowingly. "I've been a cop

long enough to know when someone's on the job. Take a break for the rest of the evening," he advised. "Don't worry, you'll find your sister's killer."

"How can you know that?"

"Because I also know 'abnormally stubborn' when I see it," he told her. "You have that look in your eyes. You'll find the killer," he repeated. "Just not today. Today is for your sister."

"So is finding her killer," Destiny countered.

Andrew laughed, shaking his head. "Like I said, stubborn. Make sure there's something left of you after you find the killer," he advised, looking at her pointedly. "Otherwise, he would have gotten two victims, not just one."

"He's right, you know," Logan told her as they watched the senior Cavanaugh retreat into the kitchen to tend to something else he was making.

Destiny sighed, then moved her shoulders in what seemed like a semishrug. "I know."

Logan wasn't fooled. He was beginning to tune in to her body language pretty well.

"That doesn't mean you're going to take his advice to heart, though, does it?"

Her first impulse was to deny his assumption, but it didn't seem quite right to lie to Logan after everything he'd done for her. For Paula. So she shook her head and told him the truth.

"Nope." With that, she began to walk away. She had people to talk to. Lots and lots of people.

Logan sighed and picked up his pace. If she was determined to do this, he wouldn't let her do it alone.

Along with her friends and coworkers at the non-profit hospital, a great many of the people whom Paula had gotten to contribute to the hospital over the years were at the reception, as well. And, it seemed to Destiny, they too felt saddened that Paula had been cut down decades before her time.

Even so, when she saw Drake Simmons, the CEO whose name she had managed to make out in the otherwise useless diary, talking to another one of the mourners, Destiny felt her pulse accelerate.

Approaching him, she forced herself to thank him for taking time out of his busy schedule to attend the service. After introducing her to Howard Palmer, his assistant, he went on to express his shock and dismay.

"Terrible thing." Drake Simmons repeated the words with such feeling Destiny was convinced that he was about to make some sort of a confession to her. Perhaps take her aside and tell her about his affair with Paula. But the man made no effort to speak to her alone, saying what he had to say in front of his assistant and Logan. "Part of me still can't believe that someone so young, so lovely and full of life is really dead."

Was it her imagination, or did his voice tremble just then?

The CEO looked at her for a moment, then confided sadly, "I just saw her recently."

How did you see her? Did you see her in the bathtub, her wrists slashed because you slashed them? Did you watch the life oozing out of her? Destiny did her best to look curious so as to urge the man on with his narrative.

"Oh?"

"Yes," he told her, his voice taking on a somber tone. "We met in my office. I wanted to give her my company's contribution personally. That children's hospital she worked for, she was their brightest star," he said with feeling. "I really don't know what they're going to do without her. Usually the people behind fundraisers turn out to be irritating, incessantly asking for more and more contributions until you wind up slamming the door in their faces—figuratively, of course."

"Of course," Destiny echoed, a smile pasted on her face.

"But Paula was different," he told her. "She made you *want* to give and give until it almost hurt." He laughed softly to himself, as if reliving some private little joke the two of them had shared. And then he cleared his throat, coming back around to the present. "I don't know about anyone else," he said, deliberately raising his voice as he looked around the immediate area, "but I'm sending a personal contribution to the hospital foundation she worked for in her memory. I hope everyone else does the same."

Destiny smiled broadly and nodded. "That's extremely nice of you, Mr. Simmons. I'm sure that Mrs. Ruben will be very grateful and will appreciate your generosity. Just as she appreciated Jacob Deering's contribution."

Simmons looked a little annoyed to be sharing the spotlight with someone else, but then a sadness seemed to overtake him as he said, "It's the very least I can do for Paula."

It was only because she hadn't wanted to turn her

sister's wake into a spectacle that Destiny refrained from verbally cornering Drake Simmons and firing questions at him until she got him to confess his affair.

More important than that, she didn't want to publicly drag Paula's name through the mud, and that would be what calling Simmons out about his affair would amount to.

The moment she was alone with Logan, she told him exactly what she was thinking. "That sounds like someone with a guilty conscience to me."

Logan tried to get her to temper her assessment by presenting another take on the scene. "Or like someone who's genuinely going to miss your sister and thought this might be a fitting tribute, donating to the hospital for whose cause she worked so diligently."

She looked at Logan sharply and frowned. "Why are you taking his side?" she asked. It was a struggle to keep her voice down.

"I'm not taking anyone's side," he countered mildly. "I'm trying to keep an open mind."

He sounded way too calm for her. Well, why shouldn't he be? she silently demanded. It wasn't *his* only sister who'd been killed.

"Don't keep it too open, or everything's going to come spilling out," she retorted.

He stared at her, trying to make sense out of what she'd just said. After a beat Logan decided that frustration and anger were shutting off the woman's ability to think clearly.

Taking her by the elbow, he directed her toward one

of the tables against the wall. Bottles of beer, alcohol and soft drinks were all there, waiting for thirsty guests.

"I think you need a drink," he told her, then specified, "Just one," in case she thought that he was attempting to get her drunk. "So you can stop being so uptight."

Her eyes narrowed and she tossed her head. "Maybe I want to be uptight," she fired back.

Logan calmly mixed vodka and orange juice together over an avalanche of ice, taking care to go heavy on the juice. After holding it up for his own examination, he was satisfied. Only then did he hand the tall, frosted screwdriver to Destiny.

"Nobody wants to be uptight," he assured her. He nodded at the glass he'd given her. "Now drink up. 'Doctor's' orders."

Doctor, her foot. He was no more of a doctor than she was. Doctor Feel Good, if anything, she thought grudgingly, taking a sip without thinking.

"Trying to get me drunk, Cavanaugh?" she challenged, raising her chin as if daring him to take a swing at her.

"No, what I'm trying to do," he replied evenly, "is to get you to relax a little. Right now, you look like you're going to snap in two any second. Either that, or do double duty as an ironing board."

"Always looking out for me." The words were said sarcastically, but he pretended not to take them in that manner.

"As long as you're working with me, yes," he answered, "I am."

Destiny looked at her new and very temporary partner over the rim of her frosty glass. The anger and the sadness within her melted into the background, as if something in his eyes had physically pushed them back.

She took a deep breath to steady her nerves. "Thanks," she murmured.

Had he not seen her lips moving, he would have sworn that he was just imagining that he heard the soft sound of her voice.

But he *had* seen them move, and he did "see" the word *thanks* on her lips. Maybe there was hope for the woman yet. That was good, because being without any hope was a horrible place to be. He couldn't begin to imagine what that had to be like. Waking up each morning without wanting to.

Without a reason to.

That had to be terrible.

Slipping his arm through hers, Logan urged, "C'mon, let's get back to 'mingling.' Lots more 'suspects' to talk to."

She got the feeling that he wasn't just teasing her, he meant it. And she was grateful to him for that.

"I don't know how to thank you," Destiny told Andrew with deep sincerity.

It was late. The reception had been over for more than an hour. The last of the mourners had left about forty-five minutes ago after once again expressing their deep sorrow over Paula's death. Drake Simmons and his personal assistant were among the last to go. Though she'd made it her mission to have their paths cross several more times throughout the day and evening, nothing new was said.

She was forced to place her impatience on hold. She had a debt to repay in some small way. She began by preparing an endless stack of dirty dishes for the dishwasher.

"You already have. Four times at last count. This makes five," Andrew told her warmly.

The next moment, he took the dish she was rinsing out of her hands. Instead of putting it into the open dishwasher, he placed it on the counter. The dishes didn't have his attention. She did.

"Go home, Destiny," he ordered. "Get some rest. You go back to fighting the good fight tomorrow." And then he turned to Logan, who had never been very far away throughout the entire day. "You might want to follow her in your car, make sure she goes home," Andrew advised after a beat.

During the course of the latter half of the reception, she'd gotten a few leads that she wanted to follow up. For her that meant getting into the precinct computer.

Logan obviously sensed that by the look on his face. Was she that transparent? she wondered.

The thought was less than pleasing. Not that she had any desire to be a woman of mystery. After all, this was her partner for now. But neither did she want to come across like a person whose thoughts were right out there for everyone to read.

"I'm going home," she assured the man who had done so much for her today and had asked for absolutely nothing in return.

She didn't like owing people, but it was, as one of Andrew's daughters—Teri, she thought—had assured her, the Cavanaugh way. Everyone just helped out everyone else without thought to compensation— or bribes.

"Of course you are," Andrew said in a tone that told her that he most certainly *did not* believe, not even for a moment, that left to her own devices Destiny would drive home and just go to bed.

It came under the heading of When Pigs Fly.

"And I know you're going home because Logan's going to follow you," Andrew concluded with a satisfied, albeit irritating, smile on his face.

"You don't have to follow me," she insisted five minutes later as she walked out of the warm house with Logan right beside her. There might be a chill in the air, but every single light seemed to be on in the Cavanaugh house, thereby generating a great deal of warmth.

Destiny's vehicle was parked close to the house. Andrew had made sure a spot directly by the front door was left for her. At the height of the reception, vehicles had littered the neighborhood for several blocks in all directions.

Now, of course, there were only a few scattered here and there, for the most part belonging to other people in the neighborhood. Everyone who had attended the reception was gone except for two of the former chief's daughters and one of his sons and their respective families.

The chief led a perfect life, she couldn't help thinking. The kind of life she would have longed to claim as her own—if her father hadn't taken that walk to buy a pack of cigarettes one fateful afternoon. Twenty years later, he still wasn't back.

"Oh, yes, I most certainly do have to follow you home," Logan told her. "I hear that when Andrew Cavanaugh makes a 'suggestion,' the person he's making it to had damn well better follow it to the letter if he or she knows what's good for them. I'm new to the family," he told her, humor curving his mouth. "I don't want to mess up. Especially not after he came through the way that he did."

Guilt. The man was wielding guilt. Great. It wasn't bad enough that she was already struggling with a megadose of it because Paula was dead and she felt that she should have been able to somehow protect her sister if only she'd taken more of an interest in her private life instead of waiting for her to share on her own. Now Logan would make her feel guilty for not doing what the former chief suggested.

"Fine, I'll go home," she said.

Logan never slowed his pace. "And I'll follow you there," he told her cheerfully.

She was going to have an escort whether she wanted one or not. For now, Destiny decided to stop fighting it.

Chapter 11

Logan remained directly behind her all the way home. There was no need to look up into her rearview mirror. She could almost *sense* that he was there.

Traffic was light. It took her less than twenty minutes to get home. After pulling up into her apartment complex, Destiny got out of her car, turned and waved at Logan. She fully expected him to wave back, make a U-turn and drive away.

But he didn't.

Instead, he found a parking space in guest parking, as it turned out not too far away from hers. Getting out, he crossed over to her.

As he approached her, with the darkness settled in all around her like an oppressive long cape, she suddenly felt vulnerable. But she had no intentions of letting him know that.

"This is a little over and above the call of duty, don't you think?" she asked when he came up to her.

"Not really. I'm sure this is what Andrew meant," he answered. Destiny noticed that once away from the gathering, Logan no longer used the "Uncle" salutation. "Besides, it's generally customary to walk a woman to her door." He nodded toward the ground-floor apartment only a few steps away.

"That's when she's your date," Destiny pointed out, adding, "I'm not your date."

"No," he agreed. "But for now, you're my responsibility."

His words stepped all over her independence. Destiny drew her shoulders back, as if preparing for a confrontation. "And just how do you figure that?"

Logan knew he had to tread lightly. She was in a bad place right now. He chose his words carefully. "Well, for better or for worse, we seemed to have been partnered up for this case, and partners are supposed to have each other's backs, especially when one partner isn't feeling one hundred percent."

Her eyes narrowed, her very stance challenging him. "Meaning me."

He inclined his head, silently agreeing with her. But when he spoke, he tempered Destiny's assumption. "For now."

Sarcasm was thick and heavy as she asked, "Would you like to tuck me into bed, too?"

"Well, then, that would have made you my date, wouldn't it?" he said, going back to her initial disclaimer. "And you're not, remember?" The smile on his

lips took on a sensual quality. "Maybe some other time."
And then Logan grew serious as he smoothed down
one side of her collar that had managed to curl under.

It was a simple, gentle gesture, and yet for some reason it threatened to bring tears to her eyes. That just
told her that she was exceedingly vulnerable beneath
the prickly words and all her efforts to appear to the
contrary.

"Are you going to be all right by yourself?" he asked.

What did he care? He had a huge family to return
to if he wanted. He had the best of all possible worlds,
and she couldn't help but envy him that.

"Or what?" she asked in a mocking tone. "You'll
sit next to my bed and read me bedtime stories until I
fall asleep?"

He laughed softly, amused by the image that conjured up in his mind. "If that's what it takes, sure, why
not?" he asked gamely.

He said it so straight-faced that for just a second,
she thought he was serious. Who knew, maybe he was.
What he said melted her defensiveness. Moreover, it
made her smile. He seemed to take everything in stride,
no matter what she said.

"You Cavanaughs are something else again," she
marveled quietly. "Even you newly minted ones."

"You didn't answer my question," he reminded her
gently. When Destiny raised an eyebrow in silent query,
he obliged her by restating the question. "Are you going
to be all right?"

For a moment, she said nothing, wondering if he
actually cared one way or another, or if he was asking

just because he felt it was expected of him. She refused to entertain the thought that it might be door number three: that he *did* care if she was going to be all right.

And then she nodded. "I'll be fine." She could see that he was waiting for her to convince him. "I don't have any other choice. Paula's killer is out there somewhere, and I intend to catch him. I can't do that if I fall apart."

"No, you can't," he agreed. "But if you need someone to talk to—or not talk to," he added with a smile that was beginning to weave its way under her skin even though she was doing her best to ignore it, "I'm available."

She nodded. That he was. To any girl with a pulse, she reminded herself. And she had never been one for team sports. "Thanks. I'll keep that in mind. But I'll be all right."

"Yeah," he said as if he had absolutely no doubt about the outcome. "You will."

She picked up the note of sincerity in his voice. He didn't have to say that. Didn't even have to be here. But he was.

"You're a good guy, Logan Cavanaugh," she told him quietly just before she impulsively brushed her lips against his cheek.

Logan felt something within his gut tighten so quickly and so hard, for a second it was difficult for him to draw in a breath.

Every fiber of his being suddenly wanted to pull her into his arms and to kiss her back. The right way. And he had a strong feeling that he wouldn't have gotten any resistance from her.

But that would be taking unfair advantage of her vulnerable state, and he didn't want things to go down that way between them. Their time would come. He was fairly certain of that now, but not tonight.

Because tonight was about healing, and she needed to do that on her terms, not his.

"Good night, Richardson," he said quietly. "I'll see you in the morning."

"In the morning," she echoed softly.

The next moment, she walked into her apartment and then closed the door behind her.

Logan turned on his heel and walked away.

It was the hardest thing he'd ever done.

And possibly the most selfless.

"You don't know how long I've waited for someone to take me seriously," Allison West said to them the next day as she sat in her living room. A huge sigh of relief accompanied the older woman's words.

Determined not to allow any more time to pass, Destiny had suggested to her partner that they interview the families of the other so-called suicide victims she'd found entered into the database.

"Debra was bright, outgoing. There was no way she would have killed herself the way the police insisted. I *know* my daughter," she said with feeling, looking from Destiny to Logan and then back again.

That was just the way she felt about Paula, Destiny thought. "The investigating detective said they found a prescription for sleeping pills near your daughter's body—" she began.

But Mrs. West was shaking her head. "That prescription wasn't hers."

"It was her name on the bottle," Logan pointed out gently.

She swung around to look at him, anger in her eyes. "I don't care what it said, I'm telling you that it wasn't hers. Debra was a personal trainer with an extensive list of clients. She really believed in what she was doing. She exercised religiously, was almost fanatical about what she put into her body. She wouldn't even take so much as an aspirin," Mrs. West insisted. "I don't know how they did it, but those pills were planted. They were not my daughter's."

Destiny tried another approach. "Can you think of anyone who might have wanted to get rid of your daughter this much?"

Again the woman could only shake her head. "No, I can't. If I knew, I would have confronted them myself, *made* them confess, even if I had to shake it out of them with my bare hands."

Given that the woman was barely five feet tall and most likely weighed as much as a pile of wet towels, her words didn't amount to much of a threat. But it was a testimony to where her heart was and how much she believed her daughter's death had been staged.

"The police said that your daughter left a suicide note, saying she was upset because she and her boyfriend had just broken up. Do you have any idea what his name was?" Destiny asked.

"No." Mrs. West's small voice hitched. "Debra wanted to keep it a secret. She said she didn't want to jinx the relationship by talking about it too soon."

Destiny stared at her, startled that Mrs. West had used the exact same words that Paula had used.

She didn't want to jinx the relationship.

"She did tell me that she thought he was perfect," Mrs. West was saying. "And that when I found out who it was, I was going to be surprised." Her eyes darkened as she took hold of Logan's wrist, squeezing it as she made her appeal. "Debra didn't kill herself. She didn't write any suicide note. It was *typed,* for God's sake," the woman cried in frustration. "Who types a note, then climbs into a bathtub and slashes their wrists? For all her outgoing nature, Debra was a very modest person when it came to her body. She wouldn't have wanted anyone to find her like that. She didn't *do* this," Mrs. West insisted again, growing progressively more agitated. "I'd stake my life on it."

Feeling compassion as well as a bond with this woman because of what she was going through, Destiny patted Mrs. West's arm. "You don't have to stake your life on it, Mrs. West. We'll find whoever did this to your daughter."

Grasping Destiny's hand between both of her own, the woman looked directly into her eyes. "Promise?" she pressed.

Destiny didn't even hesitate. "You have my word on it."

"She believed you, you know," Logan said to her when they finally left the woman's apartment some twenty minutes later.

Destiny knew exactly how committed she'd made herself. "I know."

Logan studied her profile as he asked, "And what are you going to tell her if you can't make good on that promise?"

That scenario was never going to happen, she thought fiercely. "I have every intention of 'making good' on it," she told him simply.

There was no way she could make a promise like that in good faith, and she knew it. "Destiny—"

She stopped for a moment to look at him. She knew what he was thinking. Hell, she could all but read his mind.

"Don't give me odds, Cavanaugh. We're going to get the bastard. Nothing less is remotely acceptable."

There was a fine line between being a dedicated detective and an obsessed one. "You ever read *Moby Dick?*" Logan asked as he got into the vehicle on the driver's side.

She pretended to take his question seriously. "We're not after a whale, we're after a human being. And human beings make mistakes. He will, too, if he hasn't already," she said confidently. "Somewhere, somehow, all those women I turned up have something in common. We have to find what it is."

Right. Simple, he thought sarcastically. "So, to sum up, we're looking for one needle that was in six different haystacks at one point or another."

He noted that she never even cracked a smile. "Precisely."

They returned to the precinct to review some things before planning their next course of action.

Once there, Destiny got busy compiling a file on all six of the women who had initially been thought to have committed suicide while in the throes of despair after each had supposedly broken up with the love of her life.

While she was printing up screen after screen, Logan borrowed a bulletin board and brought it into the squad room. One of the wheels had an unfortunate squeak that was heard with each complete rotation. Moving it faster only made the squeaking sound continuous, like an amorous rodent calling to its mate.

The noise drew the lieutenant out of his office and into the main area. He eyed the offensive bulletin board. "What's this?" Bailey asked.

"Visual aids," Logan told him, keeping it simple. "Richardson thought it might help if we put the victims' pictures up in chronological order with a summary of what we know about them under each."

"You mean the nonserial-killer case," the lieutenant corrected pointedly.

Logan was not about to argue with the lieutenant at this stage of the investigation. He would have needed more evidence at his disposition for that. "That's the one."

"It might not be a serial killer," Destiny said, coming up behind them. Both men turned almost in unison and looked at her quizzically. "At least, not a serial killer in the traditional sense."

"You want to explain that?" Logan requested. Seeing as how she was the one who had originally called this a serial-killer case, this was a complete one-eighty on her part and he wanted to know, in as few words as humanly possible, why she'd changed her mind.

Between arrangements for her sister's funeral and dealing with her own grief, Destiny had still managed to squeeze in some work. She'd been busy reading everything she could find on each of the other so-called nonvictims, plus she also had the benefit of the interviews she and Logan had conducted. There were still some details that bothered her. Details that didn't add up in the traditional sense.

"For one thing, I don't get a sense that our killer is enjoying this. That he's following some ritual dictates that he's unable to ignore. Most serial killers stick to a pattern religiously, one they can't deviate from, only embellish on."

Destiny looked at the photographs of the other women on the bulletin board, deliberately avoiding the last one. Her sister.

"It's almost as if the killer's doing this out of some need for expediency, like he *has* to do it *now* and quickly. And he changes things," she pointed out. "He's not slavishly bound by steps he has to follow." She pointed to one photograph, then another, moving from one pretty face to another. "One victim types her suicide note, another doesn't leave one at all. And a third sends a text message, while a fourth posts a note on her Facebook page, telling the world goodbye because 'he doesn't love me anymore.' It's like he uses whatever he can get, whatever's handy for him."

"So exactly what is it that you're saying?" the lieutenant pressed.

Frustrated, Destiny dragged her hand through her hair as she slanted a glance toward her sister's picture. The one taken at Christmas, one of the last times they'd been together. "I don't know. Just that something doesn't feel right."

Her answer did not please Bailey in the slightest. "Feelings don't stand up in court, Richardson. We need evidence. You're a crime scene investigator. You should know that," he all but barked at her.

For a second, she closed her eyes, pulling herself together. "Yes, I know that."

"Then get me some evidence!" Bailey shouted before storming away. Less than a minute later, he slammed his office door as if to underscore his order.

"Why don't we get that personal trainer's list of clients?" Logan suggested, acting as if the lieutenant hadn't even been there. "We can see if Debra trained anyone your sister interacted with. If we can just find that one point in common that they had—"

"Other than they were all in their twenties, blonde, more than reasonably attractive and supposedly committed suicide when they were 'dumped'?" she posed dryly.

"Yes, other than that."

He let his voice trail off, allowing her to fill in the silence that followed any way she wanted to. At this point, they didn't know what they were after, only that if they stumbled across it, they'd know it—if they were lucky.

"Debra West's list of clients?" Becky, the receptionist with the toothy smile repeated. She looked at them blankly for a full five seconds before saying, "We don't have a Debra West working here."

"No, you don't," Destiny agreed patiently. *Because she's dead, you idiot.* "But you did," she went on in the same calm tone. "A year ago."

"Oh. A *year* ago," she repeated as if that was the key to the secrets of the universe. "I've only been working here two months," Becky told them. "I don't know where I'd have to go to access that kind of information." She seemed perfectly happy to let the conversation drop at this point.

Sensing that she was near the end of her patience, Logan moved Destiny aside and addressed the intelligence-challenged receptionist.

"Do you think you might be able to call over someone who could possibly know how to do that?" he asked, speaking to Becky in a calm, level voice, all the while smiling into her eyes.

Whatever he was doing, Destiny noted, it had the desired effect on the receptionist.

"Sure. That would be Brittany," Becky volunteered. She jumped up to her feet as if her lower limbs had gotten the message delivered belatedly. "I'll get her for you."

"I'd appreciate that," Logan told her.

"Maybe I should have let you do the talking to begin with," Destiny murmured under her breath as Becky disappeared into the rear of the building.

"Maybe," Logan agreed, amused.

Now that he thought of it, the receptionist *did* remind him of the kind of woman he usually dated. Young, fun-loving, but definitely not a candidate for a Rhodes Scholarship in this lifetime. And, up until a few days ago, he was fairly certain that was the type he preferred and for the most part required. Because there was no chance of a meaningful or lasting relationship growing out of those sorts of liaisons.

But after trading barbs and dealing with a woman who continuously kept him on his toes, Logan began to view women like the receptionist as less appealing despite all her impressive physical attributes.

The realization, coming to him out of the blue like this, was more than just a little unnerving. It threatened to upend his world.

Just what the hell was he thinking? And why was he thinking it now?

"Something wrong?" Destiny asked as they waited for the receptionist to return with this Brittany person in tow.

Rather than answer her question, he asked one of his own, sounding, she noticed, just a little defensive. "Why do you ask?"

She shrugged, about to drop the subject when something stopped her. There was this unusual expression on his face, as if he'd suddenly realized something. About Paula's case?

"You look like you just had an epiphany," she told him.

Epiphany.

Well, that was as good a word for it as any, Logan decided.

If that indeed was what he'd just had. It sounded a lot

better than saying he'd suddenly come to his senses—
because he didn't know just how sensible he was.

"Maybe I have," he murmured more to himself than
to her.

Destiny's eyes narrowed as she tried to make sense
of what he was saying. She'd just thrown the word out
there, never once expecting him to do anything except
bristle at the term. It was a twenty-dollar word, and he
was a fifteen-dollar cop.

Was he humoring her or laughing at her?

Had he actually had an epiphany?

And why did *any* of this actually even matter to her,
she silently demanded?

*Because Paula's death knocked you for a loop and
you're trying to anchor yourself to something. And that's
understandable. But you know damn well that it can't
be him.*

No, she silently agreed, it can't be. Because a man
like Logan didn't stay for long.

Chapter 12

Logan leaned back in his chair as far as it could go. He was bone weary. It was past his shift and the squad room was empty except for him and the woman pensively staring at the bulletin board with her back to him.

Even her back looked obsessed, he thought. Where did she get her energy?

Sullivan had returned from his honeymoon, but the detective had been temporarily partnered with someone else until Logan either brought the case to a satisfying conclusion—or signed off on it. He wasn't about to give up.

He and Destiny had been at this nonstop for close to three weeks now, searching for that one common thread that connected all these so-called nonsuicides together. So far, they kept striking out.

Logan glanced over toward the bulletin board. Six

years, six women, and all they'd come up with were paralyzing dead ends.

And while he liked to think that he was a damn good detective, Logan felt as if his efforts paled in comparison to the efforts of his father's chief assistant. Richardson was there when he arrived in the morning, she was there when he left at night, eternally going over the information they'd gathered and searching for new angles, for that elusive "something" that would finally and once and for all break the case wide-open for them.

In the meantime, Logan mused, the woman *had* to be wearing herself out.

"An airline attendant, a teacher, the owner of an upscale restaurant, a wedding planner, a trainer and a fundraiser," Destiny suddenly said out loud.

Logan wasn't sure if she was addressing him or the dead women whose photographs were pinned along the top of the bulletin board.

She was reviewing their high-profile careers and frowned as she glanced at him over her shoulder. "What are we missing?"

"Right now, my best guess would be our sanity," he quipped wearily.

"Besides that," she retorted, exasperated not with him but with herself. What wasn't she seeing?

Turning back to the bulletin board, she looked at each individual photograph. The faces had begun to haunt her dreams.

"What am *I* missing?" she said under her breath.

But he'd heard her. Again he thought that Richardson was coming dangerously close to wearing herself out without even realizing it. Something had to be done before that happened.

"You want to take a break?" he asked suddenly.

"You mean like for coffee?" She was beginning to fade, she realized. Coffee might be just the thing to keep her going for another hour or so. "Sure. You can bring me back a container if you're going to the machine." She was already on to her next thought and waved in the general direction of the desk she was using. "My purse is in the bottom drawer. Take what you need."

Logan laughed to himself. "A loaded statement if I ever heard one," he commented. Richardson had handed him an absolutely fantastic straight line, and he was doing his best to be good.

Preoccupied, Destiny had only half heard what he'd said. "What?" When he didn't answer, she looked at him again. He was still sitting down. Had he changed his mind about the coffee?

"I'm talking about a *real* break," he emphasized. "Like getting away from the office—and this case—entirely. Tomorrow's Saturday," he interjected in case she'd lost track again, the way she had last Saturday—Richardson had spent the weekend at the precinct with the dead women and her computer for company, working hard and getting nowhere for her efforts.

"So?"

"So I've got a wedding to attend. My sister Kendra's getting married," he told her before she could ask. "Want to be my 'plus one'?"

For a moment, she said nothing, then decided that he had to be pulling her leg. "Don't you have a girlfriend to take?" The man, according to everything she'd heard, *always* had a girlfriend—or two—somewhere in the picture.

His mouth curved in amusement. "As my sister Kari so succinctly says, I'm in between meaningless relation-ships. And I don't want to go alone," he said, appealing to her. "Come with me."

Destiny stared at him as his words sank in. Was he actually asking her out? "A pity date? For who?" She was definitely unclear on the concept. "You, because you're in between 'meaningless' relationships, or me, because I haven't been in a relationship since slightly after the dawn of time?" Or at least it felt that way. Put on the spot, she wouldn't have been able to say just *when* her last so-called relationship had ended. It had been *that* long ago.

"How about we split the difference?" he offered gamely. "Or, if it makes you feel any better, we can say that it's for me. Your pity, my date," he said, sum-ming it up cheerfully.

Though the idea of going out with him on an unoffi-cial date was intriguing—hell, it was downright tempt-ing—she was still suspicious. "Why do you want me to come?"

"Because I think it'd do you good to get away from all this, clear your head, put things in perspective. A couple of days away from here will do you a world of good," he predicted. "And," he stressed, "because you can't keep talking to computer hardware indefinitely. Eventually, you're going to start thinking it's talking back, and then you'll *really* be in trouble."

Destiny laughed then. She didn't exactly know why, but what he'd said sounded so absurd that she had to laugh. It was the first time she'd laughed since before she'd found Paula's body.

And then, glancing one more time at the photographs that were lined up along the bulletin board so neatly, Destiny blew out a long, steadying breath.

"Maybe you're right," she allowed.

"It's been known to happen," Logan acknowledged, giving her a killer grin that she was fairly certain had melted more than its share of kneecaps. She felt her own turning slightly watery.

Her mouth curved in amusement. "Well, even a broken clock is right—"

He closed his eyes as he finished the old saying for her. "Twice a day. Yeah. I know." Opening them again, his eyes held hers for a moment. "Thanks."

She wished he'd stop looking at her like that. It made her feel completely at loose ends and unfocused. "So you're really serious about that invitation—to your sister's wedding?" As she said it, she had to admit that the idea started to appeal to her. Not that she was much of a party person, but a change of scenery for a few hours might not be completely out of order.

Logan nodded, trying his best to appear solemn rather than just dead tired. "Serious enough to come get you and drag you over to the church tomorrow whether you're ready or not."

"Then I guess I'd better be ready. What time?"

He thought for a second, trying to get the details right. "Ceremony's at eleven." He did a quick calculation backward. "I'll pick you up around a quarter after ten." And then he smiled, the expression on his face a self-deprecating one. "Kenny vividly described what she'd do to my anatomy if I show up late."

She'd met Kendra briefly at her sister's funeral. Even so, the woman had impressed her as a kindred spirit. "Is your uncle Adam officiating?" she asked.

The only way they could keep the priest from presiding over the ceremony would be to have the man kidnapped. Logan laughed. "Absolutely."

"And your uncle Andrew, is he taking care of the reception?" The latter was basically a rhetorical question.

"Who else?"

Destiny nodded. It was hard to imagine so many people being so close—but they obviously were. "A real family affair," she commented. And she truly envied him that. Especially now that she had no family of her own anymore.

Her voice, stripped of any emotion or intonation, gave him no clue as to what she was thinking—but he had a strong hunch.

"Yeah, it is."

She would have said that he was the rebellious type, not someone who conformed to the wishes of his family. And yet, here he was, sticking to the script. Just showed that you could never tell about a person.

"It doesn't get old for you?" she asked, curious.

"Hasn't been going on long enough to get old," he told her, "although, to be honest, I doubt if it ever will. They're there," he said, referring to his family members, "just enough to let you know you've got a support system if you need one, and not enough to be annoying or get under your skin."

Destiny regarded her temporary partner for a moment. He'd impressed her. "I didn't know you were that deep, Cavanaugh."

Logan shrugged off the compliment. "I didn't either." His computer already shut down for the night, Logan pushed his chair away from his desk and stood up. "I'm going to call it a night," he told her, then asked, "How about you?"

Destiny rotated her shoulders, working out a kink. "I think I'm going to stay a little while longer."

He would have bet money on that. "What a surprise," he commented dryly. Then, passing her on the way to the door, he said, "Remember, ten-fifteen, whether you're ready or not, I'm taking you to the wedding."

She thought of the clothes in her closet, and a twinge of panic momentarily telegraphed through her. "I don't have anything to wear."

He wasn't accepting excuses. "Naked might be an interesting change of pace."

"I'm serious," she called after him.

Stopping for a second, he turned around and grinned at her. "So am I." And then he relented. "I could ask Bridget to lend you one of her dresses." He did a quick assessment. "You look like you might be around the same size."

As far as she recalled, she and Bridget hadn't been anywhere near one another, so he couldn't be drawing on that to form a conclusion. "How would you know?"

He winked then and told her in a low voice, as if he

was sharing a secret, "I've got an eye for things like that."

She found herself dealing with his wink and the unexpected tidal wave it had created in the pit of her stomach. Maybe she *was* punchy.

"Don't bother your sister. I'll find something," she said dismissively.

"Don't worry. You'll look great in whatever you decide to wear."

Without thinking, Destiny pressed her hand to her stomach.

His parting words hung in the air long after he had walked out of not just the squad room but the precinct, as well.

The man knew how to make an exit, Destiny thought ruefully.

This was a bad idea.

A really *bad* idea.

The words echoed in her head the next morning as Destiny looked at her reflection in the full-length mirror on her closet door.

What was she doing, going to this wedding? She wasn't good at small talk, and she definitely wasn't in a festive mood. These people had been nice to her, and she didn't want to put a damper on the wedding by bringing anyone down.

She'd just tell Cavanaugh when he came to pick her up that she'd changed her mind. *He'll understand,* she assured herself. After all, it wasn't as if he was going to tie her down to the roof of his car and drive away.

He didn't need her as a date. The second he walked in alone into the reception, he'd have women flocking to him. Most likely, it would become a feeding frenzy.

The thought didn't ease her conscience the way she thought it would. Instead, it irritated it.

Another sign that she needed some rest. Making up her mind to stay home, she started taking off the dress that Paula had given her last Christmas. The one she'd had no occasion to wear—until now.

Or not.

There was a militant row of tiny pearl buttons from the base of her neckline to her waist on the Wedgwood-blue dress whose straight skirt stopped a few inches short of her knees. She began working them loose and had only managed to get six of them undone when she heard the doorbell.

Damn it, Cavanaugh was early. She should have known that he would be.

Biting off a few choice words, Destiny hurried to the door.

"I changed my mind," she announced as she swung it open.

Logan's deep green eyes appreciatively went from her face to an even more arresting area of her anatomy. The smile that curved his mouth would have gotten him arrested in several third-world nations.

"You've come up with something else for us to do?" he asked, his voice resonating with sensuality as well as sounding incredibly suggestive.

"No, I—" And then she remembered that she'd been unbuttoning the top of her dress, affording him a view he didn't get to see during regular hours. "You could look away," she pointed out, fumbling with the tiny buttons as she pushed them back through the loops as quickly as possible.

"I could," he agreed. "But then I'd really be missing something," he pointed out. His eyes lowered just enough to revisit the tempting, albeit disappearing view.

"Nothing you haven't seen a hundred times before, I'm sure," she said stiffly, fervently wishing that she could tamp down the flush she felt beginning to creep up her cheeks.

But she couldn't.

Nobody blushed anymore, she upbraided herself. What was wrong with her?

"Not this particular view," Logan assured her.

For a second, she was almost tempted to believe he meant it. But that would make her even more naive than she already was.

"Okay, I'm not unreasonable. We either go to the wedding, or we stay here and find another way to amuse ourselves," he said.

Her eyes narrowed. He was bluffing. "You wouldn't miss your sister's wedding."

Rather than concede that she was right, he pretended to shrug carelessly. "I have other sisters, there'll be other weddings."

Her eyes widened. "You don't mean that," she said, calling his bluff.

"What I mean," he told her seriously, "is that one way or another, I'm not leaving you alone today. How we spend the day is up to you." He looked at her pointedly.

The flash of heat came out of nowhere, telling her that if she was going to be around him, she needed at least a few other people around, as well.

Otherwise...

"All right." She surrendered. "We'll go to the wedding."

Pleased, he nodded. "Good choice. You've made my sister Kendra very happy. By the way—" he indicated her neckline with his eyes "—you missed a button."

Caught off guard, Destiny looked down at the neckline that had been plunging just a bit more than she'd intended a minute ago. "I did?"

"I could do it for you," he volunteered.

Over her dead body—then they'd never get out of the apartment.

"I see it, I see it," she said, verbally swatting him back.

Logan laughed softly to himself under his breath as he took her arm and escorted her out the door.

Some twelve hours later, they were back in front of the same door.

It might have been only half a day later, but it felt as if days, not hours, had passed by since this morning. Or maybe even a lifetime, she amended silently, smiling to herself.

It had been quite a day, at least to her.

Rather than keep to herself and sit quietly on the sidelines the way she had intended, almost immediately Destiny had found herself drawn into one conversation after another. Her opinion had been sought

out on a variety of subjects, most of which had nothing
to do with work.

Not only was her opinion sought out, but her like-
ness, as well. Despite her protest, she got pulled into
more than a few family photos. It seemed to her that
every few minutes, another camera went off and someone else framed a photograph and pulled her into it.

They were a pushy, boisterous bunch of people, and
she enjoyed their company even more the second time
around than the first. But then, this was a wedding,
not a funeral.

"I think your family now has more pictures of me
than my mother ever had in her family album."

The faded-green album she was thinking of had actually been rather sparse for what it purported to be.
Its contents spanned not just her early life but the life
of her mother and her mother's mother, as well. Three
generations and there were less than twenty pages of
photographs in total.

She shrugged carelessly as her words came back to
her. "My family wasn't much on taking pictures."

That was *not* the problem with his family, especially
not his immediate family.

Standing on her doorstep, Logan laughed. "Kari has
over twenty albums or so," he told her. "It's almost an
obsession with her."

His mind turned to more intimate things as he
watched Destiny. Even in this light, he could see her
face was ever so slightly flushed. The woman had a
slight buzz on. He would have figured she'd need more

drinks than the number she'd had to blush. Showed that you just never knew.

"So, I take it you had a good time," he guessed. Even as he made the assessment, he found himself fighting a very strong temptation a second later.

Destiny turned her face up to his and smiled.

She knew she was feeling the effects of a few glasses of champagne and that margarita—or was it two?—that she'd had a little while ago.

Better tread lightly here.

But despite her warning, she had to admit that she did like this fluttery, uninhibited feeling. And she *definitely* liked the fact that everything felt as if it was smiling inside of her.

"Yes," she told him. "I had a *very* nice time." Her eyes smiled into his. "Thanks for dragging me."

"My pleasure," he told her. It was getting harder and harder not to close his arms around her. "Anytime you want to be dragged somewhere, just let me know. I'm your guy."

I'm your guy.

Wow.

The three-word sentence stood out in blaring neon lights, completely cornering her attention.

Not that the words were true, of course. He wasn't "her guy." Why would he want to be? There were so many more exciting women for him to choose. But wouldn't it be nice if just for a moment, she could pretend that he meant it. And if…

If.

The single word that could make everything else possible, she mused.

God, now she was babbling even in her head, Destiny thought, trying to get hold of herself.

He was looking at her. Looking *into* her.

"I'm not used to partying," she heard herself saying as her throat grew progressively drier.

Amused, Logan pushed back a wisp of her hair that kept falling into her eyes. His fingertips lightly brushed against her skin.

"Really?" he teased. "You could have fooled me."

"I doubt that anything could really fool you," she murmured.

He didn't know about that. It seemed that all this time he'd been fooling himself, claiming that empty, shallow relationships were all he wanted.

That didn't seem to be enough anymore.

Not nearly enough.

The night breeze was just warm enough as it wrapped itself around them. The area was still, its inhabitants either asleep or away.

Everything seemed to be focused on the two of them.
On her.

Destiny's face was still turned up to his. A soft invitation he couldn't make himself refuse even though he knew he should.

The next moment, his lips were against hers.

And all hell broke loose.

Chapter 13

Logan wasn't sure just what he was thinking when he leaned over and kissed her. Most likely, he *wasn't* thinking.

Somewhere in the back of his mind, he had to have told himself that this would just be a simple, uncomplicated kiss. But in the depths of his soul, he had to have known better.

There was nothing simple about sharing a kiss with Destiny.

He'd already learned that the first time around. No reason to expect that the second time would be any less exhilarating.

If anything, it was more so.

Because the moment he kissed her, Logan wanted more. An entire galaxy more. He wanted to *be* with her. He wanted to *experience* her and lose himself in whatever followed.

It was as if he'd lived for years in a cave and had, just now, walked out into the bright sunlight. It might take some adjusting, but it definitely did not even begin to flirt, even remotely, with anything that was even *close* to regret.

Maybe, if Destiny hadn't kissed him back, he would have been able to harness this wild energy pulsing through him. Might have been able to get himself under control and stop after a few moments had gone by.

But she *did* kiss him back.

Hard.

And just like that, all bets were off, all the scaffolding that was carefully holding up his reconstructed walls now cracked and broke apart.

Logan's hands ran up and down along her body, increasing her body temperature until Destiny was certain she was standing in the center of a lit fireplace instead of on her doorstep.

"Hold it," she urgently breathed against his mouth as he continued to kiss her and make her head spin.

The words penetrated half a beat later, and with grave effort Logan drew back from his partner. Was she having second thoughts? Or had he misread her signals? Was he guilty of pushing too hard?

"If we keep this up out here," she told him, her words coming out in breathy spurts as she turned toward the door and did her best to stick her key into the lock, "we're going to get arrested."

So he *hadn't* misread the signs. Logan grinned. "I've

got my handcuffs in the car," he volunteered. "I could handcuff you."

He found himself talking to an empty space. Destiny had unlocked the door to her apartment and left it open for him.

"Are you coming in?"

When he didn't immediately answer, Destiny reached out, grabbed his arm and pulled him inside, impulsively taking the decision out of his hands.

"I guess I am."

His words would have been followed with a laugh, but by then, the door had slammed shut and her lips were locked onto his again. It was all he could do to keep breathing. She had a way of stealing the air right out of his lungs.

Logan could feel his body heating as an urgency surged through him.

Eager to make love to every inch of this woman, he started to undress her—or tried to. He'd forgotten about the pearl buttons running along the front of her dress. There had to be a thousand buttons in the way.

A fail-safe obstacle to allow her a last chance to reassess the situation?

"Who designed this dress?" he asked in frustration. "Nuns in some cloistered convent in the Swiss Alps?"

Destiny's heart was already beating in her throat, threatening to leap out of her body entirely. She'd never felt like this before, never experienced this level of desire before. It was all she could do to keep her whole body, including her fingertips, from trembling. This was by far the prettiest dress she owned, but in hindsight, she shouldn't have worn it.

Too late now.

"It'll go faster if we work together," she told him, her words emerging in tiny bursts of sound. "You start at the top and work your way down. I'll come in from the bottom and work my way up."

He was already doing his part, his long, slender fingers more than equal to the delicate task. "Sounds like a plan to me," he murmured, his lips and his breath grazing the side of her neck and sending shock waves through her body with every small, sexy kiss he pressed against her flesh.

The touch of his fingers against the sensitive length of the skin along her breasts generated one hell of a response within her. Yearning had multiplied in geometric proportions, and it was all she could do to keep from ripping her dress off.

But she didn't want to destroy it. She wanted to preserve it, because in a very short while, the dress—and her memories—would be all she would have left of an evening that promised to go far beyond anything she could have possibly imagined.

Their fingers brushed against one another as they both reached the very last pearl button that needed to be freed.

Destiny dropped her arms to her sides as she let him do the honors.

And when he did, slipping the back of the halter over her head, the soft blue dress floated to the floor, leaving her dressed only in his warm gaze, a pair of high heels and a scrap of white lace that had to be the ultimate minimum in undergarments.

That he didn't bother being gentle with. In a second, the undergarment was history.

The next moment, naked, Destiny was wrapped around his torso, her mouth all but hermetically sealed to his as a second wave of fire ignited between them.

He was kissing her, stroking her, touching her until she was utterly mindless. None of her surroundings registered.

They could have been in her living room, her kitchen, or on her bathroom floor for all she knew. The only things she was aware of were the all-consuming craving within her and the fact that he wasn't sating it. He was feeding it, making it grow.

And she was aware, too, of the fact that somehow, though she didn't remember if she was responsible or he was, his clothes had vanished from his body. What was beneath was tanned and toned and hard.

Doing her best to draw air into her lungs in small fits and starts, Destiny began at first hesitantly, then progressively with more confidence, to run her hands along his utterly tempting body.

Touching, teasing, stimulating.

With each pass, the thrill increased for her until it was all but unmanageable.

She wanted him with every fiber of her being, her very core moist and yearning for that final burst of fulfillment.

But even as she raised her hips to him in a silent,

sensual invitation, she discovered that Logan was intent on prolonging her experience.

Instead of driving himself into her, he took her a little at a time, making love to her body with his hands, his lips, his tongue. Creating small, lethal climaxes for her.

Even as he brought his mouth down on the hollow of her elbow, she felt a strange, wondrous miniexplosion within the center of her very core.

Her eyes flying open as her breath caught in her throat, she looked at Logan. Just what was he doing to her?

But even as she sought to ask, he'd moved on to another part of her body. And it was the same thing all over again. He was re-creating the explosions. She felt them along the slope of her throat, the swell of her breasts—first one, then the other—and then he began to move lower.

The area around her navel quivered uncontrollably with anticipation as he left a soft, hot, moist trail of intertwining kisses, working his way slowly, methodically down to his primary target.

When he coaxed her legs apart, she was certain that Logan was preparing to enter.

And he was.

But not the way she'd thought.

His breath just barely brushed along the most sensitive part of her, causing ripples of desire to seize her.

To prepare her.

Nothing could have prepared her. Not for this. Not for the sensation that followed as he lightly, subtly flirted along the outline of her femininity with just the tip of his tongue, teasing her until she thought she was going to scream.

And then he finally thrust his tongue into her.

She scrambled up eagerly to meet the explosion, her hips arched and raised as she grasped what turned out to be the sheet from her bed with both hands. She was yanking, pulling, trying to keep herself anchored to earth even as she rushed to absorb the incredible sensations that were rocking her body.

Bringing her to the edge of ecstasy and then pushing her into its swirling cauldron.

Every single part of her felt as if it was lit up and rejoicing.

And then, exhausted, spent, her body collapsed back against the mattress.

Dazed, trying vainly to somehow seal in all the delicious sensations still humming through her body, Destiny became aware that Logan was moving seductively up along her body, his body's hard ridges rubbing against her softer contours.

Arousing her all over again.

As if what had just transpired had been only an appetizer, foreshadowing the main course.

She'd thought herself completely drained, but she was wrong. From somewhere deep inside of her, a second wave of energy materialized, eagerly rushing up to meet what was about to come.

Gathering Destiny into his arms, Logan looked into the dazed wonder in her eyes for a moment, savoring it before he sealed his lips to hers.

He'd done this—made love to a woman—so many

times before that he had actually lost count. And yet, somehow, though he couldn't quite explain why even to himself, this felt different.

Was different.

The look of dazed wonder mixed with absolute pleasure in her blue eyes didn't feed his ego, didn't give him the usual sense of satisfaction that he'd done his job by pleasing his partner. Instead, the look in her eyes stirred him, excited him.

It made him want her in a way he couldn't remember wanting anyone else.

Ever.

His heart pounding hard against his rib cage, Logan pulled her closer than a breath to him.

And then he entered her.

Not with a driving force but with a measured gentleness that grew and steadily increased until the rhythm seized them both. They moved in unison to a timeless melody that grew more powerful and demanding until the final crescendo resounded and the ultimate fallout drenched them both, echoing through their bodies simultaneously, as if they truly were one.

The starbursts receded.

Logan didn't loosen his grasp, didn't draw back as the final coda faded softly into the whispers of the night. Instead, he continued to hold her, continued to savor what had just happened between them and found himself more than a little reluctant to let that sensation go, forcing him to return to earth and to reality.

He could *actually* feel her heart hammering against his. Hammering so hard that with very little effort at all, he could see the two hearts—hers and his—merging into one.

The thought lingered on his mind.

The fact that it did startled him. Since when was he given to something so sentimental? Something so, for lack of a better word, *sappy?*

What the hell was happening to him?

Having rolled off her and gathered her into his arms, Logan looked down into the face of the woman who had coaxed forward this person within him that he didn't recognize.

He wasn't certain whether to be worried that he had momentarily had some sort of a hallucination, or whether to just plain run for the hills because what had just gone on was decidedly different from anything he had ever experienced before. It had in effect exposed him to his own vulnerability, and that *couldn't* be good.

"I guess," he murmured, the words settling against the top of her head, "that you're never too old to be surprised."

Was he saying that she'd surprised him? That he hadn't thought she would be any good at this and discovering that she was had knocked him for a loop? Or was there some kind of other, hidden meaning behind Logan's words?

She was having trouble thinking clearly. All she knew was that her insides still vibrated like a tuning fork struck hard against a concrete surface.

"I surprised you?" she finally asked, needing to know. Bracing herself for his answer.

"No, *I* surprised me," he told her honestly.

He really hadn't thought that he would respond to her this way. That making love with her so completely, he'd find himself not satisfied but actually craving more.

Craving her even as his body was still warm from their first go-round.

Destiny shifted, her body brushing up against his as she looked up at him.

"I don't understand," she confessed.

Neither do I, really.

But that wasn't an answer to give her. He was supposed to be the one with all the answers. Or at least that was the way he felt.

"I'll explain it later," he promised, tilting her face up to his with the tip of his finger against her chin. Logan proceeded to lightly graze her lips with his own.

The excitement struck like lightning in a cornfield, instantly setting him on fire.

"With pictures," he added, his breath growing shorter again.

"Pictures?" she repeated, feeling her pulse once again threatening to break right through the sound barrier.

How was it that he could make her so crazy so fast? Half a second ago, she'd been too exhausted to even breathe properly. How, then, could she possibly be ready to go at it again with him?

But she was ready. Oh, so ready, as anticipation hummed in her veins.

"What kind of pictures?" She pushed the words out with difficulty, all of her focused on the explosions gathering within her throbbing body.

Excitement swiftly moved through her, filling every nook with sunshine.

"Pretty ones," he told her with effort.

Or, at least he *thought* he told her.

He definitely couldn't swear to it because his mind was, even now, retreating, losing the ability to form even simple complete thoughts.

All that was there now was desire, once again growing to gigantic proportions and promising to be even more unwieldy the second time around.

Which was more than all right with him.

It was the very last semicoherent thought Logan had for a long, long time.

Chapter 14

Destiny was fairly sure that what had happened between Logan and her that evening after his sister's wedding was a one-shot deal.

Well, technically, it was a three-shot deal, she'd corrected herself, because they'd made love a total of three times by the time Sunday-morning light had crept into her bedroom.

She had a feeling that Logan pretty much felt the same way.

Given that, it was rather difficult to estimate which of them was more surprised when Sunday began to take on the same qualities of the night before.

They were making love less than five minutes after they woke up.

Destiny wasn't even sure just how it started, only how it ultimately wound up. She'd even, for a few seconds before she'd become aware that Logan was awake, started to think about the case.

Or rather, she'd realized that something in the back of her mind was bothering her about the case. Something elusive nagging at her that she felt she should have caught by now.

But before she could fully concentrate on trying to summon it to the foreground and begin to explore exactly *what* was bothering her, her body was otherwise engaged, sending her mind back into the netherworld.

"You know," Logan told her a little while later as he collapsed beside her on the bed and another exquisite marathon lovemaking session between them had taken its place in history, "we just might be setting some kind of record here."

It took her a moment to pull enough air into her lungs to be able to answer him. "Well, I know that this is certainly *my* personal best."

The moment the words were out, Destiny realized she'd just shared too much information. On the one hand, it seemed rather silly to feel awkward about what she'd just told him. After all the man had now seen her naked for the better part of three-quarters of a day.

But on the other hand, a month ago she had not even *known* him well enough to say hello to him when she passed him in the hall. Other than the fact that he was Sean's son, Logan had been a stranger to her.

He certainly isn't a stranger now, is he?

No, he wasn't. But, other than being her temporary partner for this case, she really didn't know *what* Logan was.

Logan had propped himself up on his elbow and was looking down at her face. The smile on his lips went straight to the place responsible for taking memories and pressing them between the pages of time, to remember and treasure for as long as possible.

"I certainly have no complaints on my end," he assured her softly.

Destiny could feel desire stirring within her. Again.

Okay, this was just impossible. How could she have turned into this insatiable, love-hungry creature after all these years of doing without and getting along just fine? she silently demanded. Until yesterday, she'd been completely convinced that she didn't need this kind of reaffirmation, that sex was something she could easily do without, thank you very much.

Now, given a choice of lovemaking or breathing, she would have gravitated toward the former without a second thought.

He was making her want him just by *looking* at her, for heaven's sake. Just by smiling at her. Not to mention that feeling his breath on her skin was making everything quicken inside her.

She needed to get up, to start moving, to distance herself from this man who had such power over her, Destiny told herself.

Otherwise, she was just going to jump his bones again. It was only a matter of time.

"I'm going to make us breakfast," she announced, sitting up. "You hungry?"

"Yes," he answered, his eyes on hers, his voice so low it seemed to softly ripple along her skin.

He wasn't talking about food, Destiny thought, her stomach muscles quivering. She thought about rallying, about resisting.

And then she stopped thinking altogether.

"Oh, the hell with it," she cried, surrendering.

Logan yanked her back down onto the bed. "My thoughts exactly," he agreed just before he brought his mouth down on hers.

And just like that, they set each other's worlds on fire again.

Destiny congratulated herself on getting better at giving back as good as she'd gotten, taking things that Logan had done to rock her world and using them to do the same to his. A sense of euphoria wove itself through her.

As the final climax seized her, it was all Destiny could do not to yell out Logan's name. But the sensation, rather than bursting apart and then fading, insisted on building, taking her up even farther than she'd already gone with him those other times.

Exhausted, drained and contented beyond words, she focused on the hard task of just breathing.

Cocooned in the vanishing embrace of ecstasy, she had absolutely no idea why this extraneous thought had come out of nowhere and engaged her brain.

If, propelled by a need to know, she had attempted to explore its origins, she might have said that her own lovemaking experience had made her more sympathetic to her sister, to what Paula must have felt when she suddenly found herself abandoned by the man she had planned to be with for the rest of her life, and *that* was why her mind kept returning to the case.

"Cell phone!" Destiny cried suddenly just as the euphoria faded.

Spent, Logan turned his head and looked at her quizzically. "Well, that's a new one. I don't think anyone has ever yelled that out when they've climaxed."

Her brain, still in a haze, was going three different directions at once, and his comment only confused her. "What?"

"You just yelled out 'cell phone,'" he told her. "Is that your new nickname for me, or were you just thinking of calling someone while we were...?"

Embarrassed, she covered her face with her hands. "No. Oh, God, no," she cried.

And then it began coming together for her. She could slowly make sense of everything, especially the blurry, elusive thought that had nagged at her.

Destiny bolted upright in the bed, the light blue top sheet pooling about her waist. For the moment, she was completely oblivious to the fact that she was naked from the waist up.

She grabbed Logan's wrist as she talked, as if to pull him into her thought process.

"We've cross-referenced all the people the six dead women worked with, all the people they socialized with, the churches they went to, and none of it has turned up a link."

He could see that she was going somewhere with

this. "Keep talking," he encouraged, waiting for the bottom line.

That was just the problem. She knew if she let herself, she'd start rambling, pulling in sidebars. Destiny forced herself to focus.

"Okay, if you have a lover who wants to remain out of the spotlight, in order to humor him you wouldn't have his name anywhere that someone else could discover it, like on a list of clients." The last was a direct reference to Debra West's list of people she worked with as a trainer.

"Makes sense," he agreed, still waiting for Destiny to get to her "eureka" moment.

"But you do want to be able to get in contact with him whenever you want to talk to him or see him, right?" She didn't wait for Logan to agree. "So, what would be the harm in having his number programmed into your cell phone?" she posed.

Her question gave birth to another question in his mind. "Is that what you did?"

She hadn't seen that one coming. For a moment, to save her pride, Destiny was going to say something flippant, or just say "yes" and move on with her point, but that would be lying and she didn't want to lie to him. Besides, lies had a way of tripping you up.

So she shrugged and told him the truth. "I've never had a lover I wanted to reach at a moment's notice." That still conveyed the wrong message, and she knew it. That sounded as if she'd had lovers before, but those men in her past, they had just been casual relationships.

She didn't want Logan thinking something that wasn't true. "I've never actually had a serious lover before."

That surprised him. He looked at her for a long moment before finally asking, "So that makes me your first?"

"In a manner of speaking, yes." She wasn't a virgin. She figured he was experienced enough to realize that. But, if there was such a thing, in the past few years she'd become practically a virgin—until last night.

Wait—what was he saying? She looked at him, her surprise and confusion registering plainly on her face. "Are you saying that you're my lover, or just that we made love?" She needed to get that straight. It might not make a difference to him, but it made all the difference in the world to her.

"Yes," he answered, deliberately leaving it ambiguous for now. And then, before she could ask anything further, the detective in him stepped to the foreground. "But I think you have something there with the cell phone."

She knew she did. It only made sense. She knew Paula. Paula would have wanted to be able to reach the man she was involved with whenever she could.

Thinking out loud, Destiny said, "What we need is to get the records of all the dead women's cell phone calls for, let's say the last three months before they were killed, and what we *really* need is someone who can come up with a program that will cross-reference all the calls our victims made to see if there's a phone number that shows up on all six phones."

From where she stood, that sounded like an incredibly daunting task that, undertaken manually, would make a person cross-eyed and send them running to an optometrist within a matter of a day. But it didn't need to be done manually.

"You have access to anyone like that?" he asked.

Destiny grinned, surprised that he didn't know the answer to that. "Your cousin Dax's wife, Brenda. She can make a computer roll over, sit up and beg in less than sixty seconds."

He'd heard his father mention the name a couple of times, but to be honest, he hadn't been paying all that much attention. He hadn't realized that the woman was a computer wizard *or* a relative, although the latter was by marriage.

"We don't need it to beg," he told her. "We just need it to come up with a common phone number."

"That, too," she promised. Excited, she said, "I think we're finally getting somewhere."

Logan liked the way her eyes danced when she was excited. He surprised her by pulling her back down onto the bed and then beneath him.

"I'm counting on it," he told her, his voice a deep, sexy whisper.

There went her heart again, skipping beats and pounding madly in between.

And in that heart, she knew that as lovely as this interlude with Logan was, it was only temporary. Maybe even just for the weekend, no matter how beguilingly he talked.

Which meant that she needed to savor every second of it before it no longer was.

"It's Sunday," she told him, her body heating as he pressed a kiss to the side of her neck. "I can call her later."

"Good idea," he agreed, getting back to the earnest, all-consuming endeavor of making love with her for as long as he had a breath left within him.

The way he saw it, it was a noble ambition and one hell of a way to go.

It took Brenda less than twelve hours after she was presented with the challenge to come up with a program that could take all six lists of cell phone numbers called and cross-reference them against one another.

And in exactly twelve hours and thirty-nine minutes, Logan and Destiny had their linking phone number.

"Do you know who it belongs to?" Logan asked the chief of detective's daughter-in-law.

Brenda grinned. "Is the pope Catholic? The number belongs to Drake Simmons. It's apparently his private number." Then, in case they didn't know, Brenda added, "He's a big-shot CEO with—"

Destiny cut her short. "Yes, we know," she said between gritted teeth. And to think that he'd had the nerve to look so mournful at Paula's funeral. "He spoke to me at her funeral and told me to call on him at any time if there was any way that he could help us find Paula's killer."

"Apparently, it looks like he's in a good position to point him out to you," Brenda surmised.

Nodding, disgusted, Destiny was in a hurry to get going. "Thanks, Brenda, you're the best."

Brenda flashed her a grin. "Of course I am. Now, if you'll excuse me, I've got a stack of emergencies all waiting to be first." She was already turning her attention to the next case as Destiny and Logan walked out.

"Let's go get the bastard," Destiny said, seething.

"Let's see just how he's connected to all the other women before we go paying Mr. Simmons a visit," Logan advised.

He wanted to be able to make this stick, and he knew she did, too, but she was letting her emotions get the better of her. Not that he could really blame her. If it had been one of his sisters who had been murdered, he knew he would have gone off half-cocked himself. Which was why detectives had partners.

"I don't want to 'talk' to him," Destiny retorted angrily as she walked toward the elevator. "I want to beat him to a pulp."

"Talking first," he emphasized. "And then we'll see about the beating part."

She knew he didn't mean it. Most likely, he knew she didn't either. That she was just blowing off steam, just talking. But for the first time in her life, the thought of physically beating someone did not leave her repulsed. Drake Simmons had killed her baby sister, and she wanted to make him pay for it. She wanted to hurt him.

Being civil to this man who'd made such a show of wanting to help bring Paula's killer to justice, all the while knowing that he was the one responsible for killing her, would not be easy.

As if sensing the turmoil within her, Logan looked at her just before they got on the elevator. "You going to be all right?" he asked.

No, I'm not going to be all right. I may never be all

right. Paula's dead, and that preening Cheshire Cat killed her.

But that, she knew, wasn't what Logan wanted to hear, and if she told him that he'd find a way to stop her from coming with him.

So instead, she said, "Once we nail this son of a bitch and he's in jail, I'll be just peachy."

There was sarcasm if he'd ever heard it, he thought. And he had a feeling that he had his work cut out for him.

Once they knew that Simmons was the "mysterious lover" whom each of the six women were involved with before their untimely deaths, finding the exact connection proved to be easy.

Five years ago, Adele Atkins, the flight attendant, had been on duty on a trans-Atlantic flight that Simmons had taken. Their affair started the moment the plane landed.

Four years ago, Barbara Watson had been his son's junior high school math teacher, and they'd met on back-to-school night. Apparently, what he'd met at back-to-school night he'd taken back to his love nest. That lasted six months before it abruptly ended. Her "suicide" followed in less than a week after the affair was over.

Jennifer Bedlow was next. She was the wedding planner three years ago who handled his daughter Margaret's wedding and was in turn *handled* by Simmons for what appeared to be four months before that, too, ended, only to be shortly followed by her death three days later.

Two years ago Eloise Jorgansen was the hands-on

owner of what was, for nine months, Simmons's favorite restaurant. And then he just stopped going there.

A year ago Debra West had taken Simmons on as her "special" client, training him in private whenever he called, day or night. For that she was paid twice her going rate before she, too, joined the suicide brigade.

And last but definitely not least, Paula had met and apparently fallen for Simmons while asking him to have his company contribute a sizable sum to the Children's Hospital of Aurora.

At first glance, Simmons had very aboveboard reasons for his initial interaction with all these women. It was only when the interactions became intensified and exclusive that things began to look questionable.

And she had just the questions she wanted to ask him once they brought Simmons in.

I'll get him, Paula, she silently promised as she got into the department vehicle beside Logan, who was driving. *He's going to pay for what he did to you, I swear.*

The polite greeting and tight smile Drake Simmons offered when Logan and Destiny were brought into his office quickly faded when the nature of their visit became clear.

Stunned, he could only repeat what he'd just been told. "You're accusing me of killing Paula? Are you out of your minds?" Simmons thundered in a voice that made his underlings quake. "She was a wonderful woman. I would have *never* hurt Paula."

"This went beyond hurt," Destiny bit off, tired of the virtual hide-and-seek game they were playing. "You had an affair with my sister, and when you got tired of her, the way you got tired of all the other women before her, you found that she wasn't going to go quietly. That made her a liability to you and that perfect little world you lived in, so you killed her."

Obviously, Simmons had had enough. "Get out, both of you," he ordered. Then, glaring at Destiny, he added, "You are insane."

"And you are under arrest," she fired back. She glanced in Logan's direction, fully expecting him to back her up. "Put the cuffs on him, Cavanaugh."

Her eyes on Simmons, she was positive she had the right man. His prints were found in Paula's apartment, and she was fairly confident if they showed his photograph to the pharmacist where the sleeping pills had been obtained, the man would ID Simmons as the person who paid for that medication.

"You have the right to remain silent," she recited. "If you give up that right, what you say can and will be held—"

"All right, all right," Simmons cried, pulling away before Logan could secure the handcuffs on his wrists. "I had an affair with your sister," he admitted angrily, "but that's not a crime."

"Killing her is," Destiny snapped.

"I didn't kill her!" Simmons shouted desperately.

Her face was expressionless as she looked at the CEO. "Convince me." It was an order.

Simmons no longer projected cool confidence. Instead, he looked like a man who'd been cornered—and was terrified.

"Tell me what time she was killed." There was a frantic edge to his voice. "And I'll tell you where I was."

When Logan gave the CEO an approximate time of

death, Simmons hesitated for a few seconds, trying to recall his whereabouts that day.

"Wait a minute," he cried. "Let me just call in my assistant—"

"So he can lie for you?" Logan asked knowingly. He wouldn't have been the first high-powered man who'd convinced an underling to take the fall for him.

"No, so he can bring me my schedule. He makes all of my appointments. Howard knows my schedule better than I do."

"And this schedule," Destiny wanted to know, "does it go back five years?"

Simmons paled beneath his very expensive tan. "Why?"

"Because it seems that all the dead women have your private cell phone number programmed into their cell phones."

Pressing the button that connected him to his assistant, Simmons requested that Howard bring the schedule in quickly.

"Make sure you bring in my schedule for the last five years," he emphasized nervously just before releasing the button on the intercom and turning toward Logan and Destiny.

"I know how this looks," he said in a voice that was no longer arrogant but subdued and possibly just a little fearful. "But I didn't kill any of those women. I'm not a monster."

"We'll see" was all Destiny trusted herself to say for now.

Chapter 15

Still handcuffed, Drake Simmons was brought in, then booked and fingerprinted, all while angrily protesting his innocence and demanding to see his lawyer.

"When last seen, your assistant, Howard, was trying to locate your lawyer for you," Logan told the man evenly. "Meanwhile, rather than sending you off to a holding cell in our jail, we've arranged for you to wait in one of our interrogation rooms."

Logan knew it would be just a short matter of time before the CEO's lawyer would post bail for the man. Though he couldn't legally question him, there was always a chance that Simmons, in his anger, would let something unintentionally slip, so it was better to have the man close by than in lockup.

Logan looked at the policeman who'd escorted Simmons down to booking and back. "Put Mr. Simmons in interrogation room three and see that he stays there," he instructed.

Just as Simmons was taken away, Sean Cavanaugh walked into the squad room.

"Dad," Logan said, surprised to see his father. He could count on the fingers of one hand the number of times he'd seen the man out of the lab at the precinct. "What are you doing above the first floor?"

"I came to see if my chief assistant needed some moral support." He looked over toward the desk where Destiny was sitting. "Word has it that you made an arrest on the case."

Getting to her feet, Destiny quickly made her way over to her boss.

"We did," she confirmed. There was no pride in her voice, no indication that the battle was finally over.

Sean had always been able to read people. It was one of the reasons he'd gone into the line of work that he had.

"I sense a 'but' in the air. How airtight is your case?" he asked, looking from his son to Destiny. "What kind of evidence do you have?"

"Circumstantial," Destiny was forced to admit, but she quickly assured the older man, "But there's a ton of it. Simmons's fingerprints are at her apartment, and there are dozens of cell phone calls between them in the week before she died, not to mention too many to count over a period of eight weeks."

Sean shook his head very slowly. "That just proves that they knew each other, not that he killed her," he pointed out quietly.

She didn't want to hear any negative arguments. "He did it, Sean. He's responsible for Paula's murder. I can *feel* it," Destiny insisted.

Sean was nothing if not sympathetic. Although he placed a great deal of emphasis on black-and-white evidence, he also believed that at times, investigators had to go with their gut feeling.

"Then go for it," he urged. "And you—" he turned toward Logan "—help her." It was a direct order, not from a father to his son but from the head of the crime lab to a detective.

"That's what I've been doing, Dad," Logan replied. He wasn't defensive in his answer. There was no need to be. His father knew him well enough to know he didn't lie.

Sean nodded, as if he knew that but had just wanted to hear it said out loud—predominantly for Destiny's benefit.

Simmons's lawyer as well as his assistant arrived less than half an hour later. The delay had been unavoidable because it had taken Simmons's assistant, Howard, that long to find the sections from the CEO's schedule that had mysteriously gone missing.

The printout copies were now safely in Logan's hands, and the pages showed that Simmons had been clear across town, at another hotel room with his latest love interest at the time of Paula's death.

The man was disgusting, Destiny thought as she looked over the pages that provided Simmons with

an alibi. He'd no sooner cut her sister loose than he'd
hopped into bed with someone else.

Howard took the opportunity to preen before the police department duo. It was obvious that he was enjoying rubbing their noses in his boss's innocence.

"So Mr. Simmons couldn't have been in that woman's apartment, drugging her and slashing her wrists
before putting her into the bathtub," Howard crowed
as he haughtily looked down his nose at Destiny and
Logan. "You're just going to have to pin this on somebody else."

It had almost gone sailing over her head.

Said so quickly by the little man, his words had almost not registered.

But then they did.

And when they did, they wound up hitting her like
the proverbial ton of bricks.

Stunned, Destiny exchanged glances with Logan to
see if he'd picked up on it, as well. Judging by his de-
layed reaction, the all-important phrase had taken the
long way around getting to her partner, as well.

"Would you mind repeating what you just said?"
Logan requested politely.

"You people deaf as well as blind?" Howard demanded nastily. "I *said* Mr. Simmons can't be blamed
if that two-bit floozy pumped herself full of drugs and
then slashed her wrists. He has important work to do.
He's not her guardian angel, you know."

"Nobody would accuse him of being that, that's for
sure," Destiny couldn't help saying with more than a
little contempt in her voice. "But then, someone might

just turn the tables and accuse *you* of killing Paula," she said, suddenly getting into the man's face.

"Me?" Paling, his eyes growing wider and wider, Howard croaked out a protest. "You're crazy, you know that? Absolutely freakin' crazy!"

"Oh, I don't know. That little detail about the drugs found in Paula's system, that was left out of the media story. As a matter of fact, from what I'd read in the other files, that salient point was left out of the articles about *all* the dead women. How is it that you were aware of that information, Mr. Palmer?" Destiny asked pointedly.

A little uneasy, Howard shrugged his sloping shoulders. "I dunno. I must have read it somewhere."

"You're not paying attention, Howard," Destiny told him. She could barely contain her excitement. They might have lost Simmons as a suspect, but Howard was shaping up rather nicely to fill that vacant slot. "That little fact was kept from any and all media. It's our ace in the hole, the let's-see-who-knows-more-than-they're-telling card. No one knew about the drugs in the women's systems except for the investigating detectives and the medical examiner—and the man who killed her." Her eyes narrowed as she leaned in over the table. "Which right now would seem to be you."

"No," he insisted, his voice going up an octave. "You're making a mistake."

"From where I'm standing, you're the one who made the mistake, Howard," she stated.

"You're just trying to pin this on someone!" he accused, then pulled himself up to his full five-foot-five height. "And I've had enough of these accusations. I'm going home."

But as he began to walk toward the door, Logan rose to his feet and all six foot three of him blocked the other man's path.

"I'm afraid I can't let you do that, Howard. It looks like you're going to have to be the guest of the city for a while." His eyes held the other man's. "With any luck, for a very long while."

Real panic seemed to set in as Simmons's personal assistant wobbled on his feet.

"You can't put me in lockup. There's nothing but lowlifes there." Breathing hard, he declared, "You're bluffing. You're just looking to pin these murders on someone," he repeated indignantly.

"Actually, yes, we are," Destiny agreed, then clarified, "The *right* someone, and you now seem to be even a better candidate than your boss. So tell me, how did this play out?" she asked, her voice growing harsh. "He has the good time and when he's done, you get to clean up after him? Does he *pay* you enough for that kind of thing?" she demanded.

Howard Palmer did nothing but whimper.

Splaying her hands on the scarred surface, Destiny leaned over the table, her face inches away from Palmer's. "You realize that this way, he gets to have an alibi and your fingers, so to speak, are all over the crime. He's dumping this all on you, Howard. Without your testimony, he gets to walk and you get the execution chamber. You're the fall guy, Howard." Still inches away from him, Destiny whispered urgently, "Don't let him do this to you."

But Palmer shook his head so hard, some of the sweat from his forehead flew off and managed to make contact with her face.

"You've got this all wrong," he cried. "All wrong. Mr. Simmons never asked me to do anything except offer his ex-girlfriends money, something to tide them over until their lives got back on track. He was never anything less than a gentleman."

Was that what passed for a gentleman these days? Well, not in her book, not by a long shot.

"Right, he's a regular prince," she spat out. "So, what are you saying here, Howard?" Destiny asked the man sharply. "You read between the lines and did what you *thought* Simmons wanted you to do?"

The man blew out a shaky breath as he stared up at the ceiling. He seemed to be hoping that a black hole would open up and swallow him.

Finally he said in a small, still voice, "I did what had to be done."

Logan could see that the second the words were uttered, they'd waved a red flag in front of Destiny. He indicated to her to let him continue asking the questions. They needed a confession, and they needed someone calm to go after it. Right now, that wasn't her.

"And exactly what had to be done, Howard?" Logan pressed.

"The threat had to be eliminated," Howard said, a desperate, pleading edge back in his voice.

"What threat?" Destiny asked. This wasn't making any sense. Her sister had never been a threat to anyone.

"Why, to Mr. Simmons's good name, of course," the assistant insisted, as if that was elementary and as plain as day. "If one of those whores decided to sell her story to one of those tabloid rags, his career chances would be over."

Destiny and Logan exchanged looks. Simmons had climbed up as high in his company as a man could go. "I'm afraid you lost us, Howard," Logan told him, then asked, "What career chances?"

Fidgeting, Howard sighed impatiently, as if trying to suffer through dealing with imbeciles. "It hasn't been made public yet, but Mr. Simmons has been planning for years on running for senator. If word got out about his insatiable sexual appetite—"

"Most likely he'd fit right in with the Washington crowd," Logan concluded cynically.

But Howard disagreed. "Mr. Simmons needed a spotless record. He might not have realized that, but I did," he said importantly. "He has a wife, a family. If his affairs came to light, he might not get elected."

It was beginning to come together. Destiny felt outraged as well as sick to her stomach.

"So you're telling us that you killed all those women just to protect Simmons's good name?" Destiny asked incredulously.

"Someone had to," Howard insisted with passion.

"And Simmons never asked you to do any of this? Not even indirectly?" Logan asked.

"Mr. Simmons, I'm ashamed to admit, was usually

already involved with someone else and not thinking about any woman who had come before." Howard pressed his lips together. "Mr. Simmons doesn't walk away from one woman without having his sights set on another one."

"A game plan, how very organized of him," Destiny bit off sarcastically. She rose from her chair. "Well, I think we've got enough on him to make this stick."

Logan was already on his feet. "I totally agree," he responded.

Howard looked from one interrogator to the other and then back again, his head all but spinning. "Make what stick?" he asked nervously, his voice rising and cracking on the last word.

"Oh, you're a smart man, Howard," Destiny told him in a syrupy voice. "I think you can figure it out." And with that, she walked out of the room with Logan right behind her.

Howard began to yell after them, but she made no effort to listen, or to turn around and walk back in. As far as she was concerned, her work here was done. She'd lived up to her promises, both her silent one to her sister and to the verbal one she'd given Mrs. West about bringing the woman's daughter's killer to justice.

"Take him down to booking," Logan told the detective they'd left posted outside the interrogation room.

The detective looked more than happy to comply.

Destiny sighed as she leaned back in the passenger seat. After making sure that everything was in order and all the right reports were filed, she and Logan were finally calling it a night and leaving the precinct.

It had been a long, long day, and she was more than tired. But happy. Very, very happy. And then it hit her. Right between the eyes.

It was over.

She'd found the man who had killed not just her sister, but also five other women. There was no need for her to hang around the squad room any longer.

And that was when the full implication of that hit her, as well. She could go back to the crime lab. Her work was done.

And so were they.

Out of sight, out of mind, right? And if she needed any proof of that, all she had to do was look at the life expectancy of any one of Logan's affairs. It gave new meaning to the words *short-term*.

It was probably over already. He might just drop her off at her door and not come in. Or, if he did, it would be just "one last time" and then they—she—would be history.

She'd been way too quiet, Logan thought. Not that the woman had ever been exactly a chatterbox, but this was eerily silent, even for her.

"You know," he said, glancing at Destiny as they came to a red light and stopped, "for a woman who just nailed the guy responsible for killing her sister, not to mention five other women, you sure don't look very happy."

"Oh, I'm very happy," she protested.

He shifted his foot off the brake and back onto the

accelerator. "If that's very happy, remind me to run for the hills when you're being very sad."

Right, as if he was going to stay one more second than he had to. "Don't worry, you won't be around to see that."

"Why?" he pressed. "Where am I going to be? You know something I don't?" Had there been some sort of a shake-up in the department he hadn't heard about? He had a habit of ignoring memos and email communications, which at times made him the last to know about precinct matters.

"I'll be going back down to the crime lab."

"Okay." He drew the word out, waiting for more, for some sort of enlightenment.

Annoyed, she blew out a breath. "And you'll be up here."

Still no enlightenment. "So? You're talking about four floors, not scaling the Himalayas or going halfway around the world."

"It might as well be that."

Okay, he needed to call her on this since she obviously wasn't going to volunteer anything remotely close to plain talk unless he deliberately *asked* her to.

"I've got three sisters, Richardson. I know all about sideways thinking and stuff coming out of mouths that make absolutely no sense to the male mind. I've always been good at putting the pieces together and solving puzzles, but I've got to admit you have me completely stumped. Just what the hell are you talking about?"

She stared straight ahead into the darkness as he

approached her apartment complex. "You don't have to pretend."

"Pretend what? That I'm confused?" he guessed when she didn't say anything. "This isn't pretending. I am *really* confused. What are you talking about?" Logan asked again.

She looked at him. "You don't know what I'm talking about," she said sarcastically.

Finally, at least they'd established that. "Hell, I haven't got a *clue* what you're talking about."

Now he was getting her angry. Did he think she was simpleminded? "I'm talking about moving on."

Pulling up into a space in guest parking, he turned off the ignition and looked at her, stunned. Where had this come from? He'd thought they were doing well. Progressing, even. And now she hit him with this. "You want to move on?"

Oh, God, *why* was he doing this to her? Torturing her this way? They both knew what she was like. "No, *you* want to move on."

He stared at her as if she'd lost her mind. And then a trickle of relief began to flow through him. "Well, if I do, I haven't told me yet, so let's just keep that a secret."

"This isn't funny, Logan," Destiny insisted, glaring at him.

"*Finally.* Something we can agree on."

For just a second, she was speechless. Was he saying that…?

No, this was Logan Cavanaugh, a man who'd refused to have any ties outside his family. For some reason, he was playing mind games with her. Well, no more beating around the bush. She intended to resolve this head-on. She couldn't take nurturing false hopes.

"You're telling me that you don't want to move on."

He never blinked as he repeated, "I'm telling you that I don't want to move on."

So maybe she had a little more time with him, but that didn't change what was eventually coming, and she knew it. They *both* knew it.

"Yet," she said.

"Ever," he countered.

No, no, she couldn't let herself get sucked in. She couldn't allow herself to believe that he was talking about something permanent.

And yet...

Her voice was far less confident and a little shaky as she began, "So you're telling me—"

He didn't want to go another round of trading barbs or having her toss accusations at him. He couldn't blame Destiny for being skeptical. He figured she knew all about his reputation. Hell, everyone knew all about his reputation.

But this had nothing to do with his reputation and everything to do with his new view on what life should *really* be about. About having the same person beside you, the same person to love and share things with, good *and* bad.

"That I love you and I intend to stick around until you toss me out," he said, concluding what he knew she hadn't been about to say.

Every inch of her was tingling now. It began to dawn

on her that he just might be serious. "And if I don't toss you out?"

His smile was almost radiant. "Then I become a permanent fixture in your life."

Everything inside of her was holding its breath, wanting so desperately to believe what he was saying. At the same time, she was afraid to believe it.

"How permanent?" she asked, her voice a low whisper.

"Permanent-permanent." He brushed his fingertips along her face, exciting both of them. "Bonding cement permanent. World-without-end permanent." The urge to kiss her was tremendous, but this had to be put to bed first. "Convinced yet?"

Her mouth was cotton dry. "Not yet. I'm still working on stunned."

"You work on 'stunned,'" he told her, moving aside the hair against her neck and then touching his lips to her skin. "I'll work on you."

Her eyes fluttered shut as delicious sensations sprang up, fully grown and raring to go. "You know I can't think when you do that."

She felt him laugh against her skin. Who would have thought that could excite her, as well? But it did. Very much.

"That's the whole idea," he told her, pressing another kiss to her neck. Sending shimmies of desire through her. "You've done entirely too much thinking. Time to bring your senses into play."

It was hard to think. Harder to talk, but she had to

tell him this. "Well, before my senses start playing, I just want to tell you that I love you, too."

"I know."

She drew back to look at him. How could he know when she'd just really found out herself? The moment he'd said he loved her, something strong and kindred had leaped to the foreground within her.

"You know?"

He nodded and there was that sexy smile again, completely turning her to mush inside. "Your eyes gave you away."

She laughed softly, finally beginning to relax, to feel that it was going to be all right. "I didn't realize you were a student of eyes."

He raised one shoulder in a careless shrug. "Eyes, lips, nose, vital body parts—I'm a student of everything there is to study and know about you. Now, if you don't mind," he went on, his eyes teasing her, "I've fallen behind in my homework and I need to catch up."

There it was again, that thrill of anticipation. "Far be it for me to keep you from your homework."

He laughed then and she hugged the sound to her. Getting out of the car, he rounded the trunk—or half the trunk.

They met in the middle.

"That's my girl."

"Yes," she told him, entwining her arms around his neck, "I am."

It was the start of a record-breaking kiss.

Logan had intended to ask her to marry him, but he

realized that she might not be ready to hear that just yet.
That was all right. It would keep. He could be patient.

But not too patient, he thought as the kiss intensified.

Maybe he'd ask her in the morning.

It sounded good to him.

* * * * *

REQUEST YOUR FREE BOOKS!
2 FREE NOVELS PLUS 2 FREE GIFTS!

 Harlequin®

ROMANTIC
SUSPENSE

Sparked by Danger, Fueled by Passion.

YES! Please send me 2 FREE Harlequin® Romantic Suspense novels and my 2 FREE gifts (gifts are worth about $10). After receiving them, if I don't wish to receive any more books, I can return the shipping statement marked "cancel." If I don't cancel, I will receive 4 brand-new novels every month and be billed just $4.49 per book in the U.S. or $5.24 per book in Canada. That's a saving of at least 14% off the cover price! It's quite a bargain! Shipping and handling is just 50¢ per book in the U.S. and 75¢ per book in Canada.* I understand that accepting the 2 free books and gifts places me under no obligation to buy anything. I can always return a shipment and cancel at any time. Even if I never buy another book, the two free books and gifts are mine to keep forever.

240/340 HDN FEFR

Name _____ (PLEASE PRINT)

Address _____ Apt. #

City _____ State/Prov. _____ Zip/Postal Code

Signature (if under 18, a parent or guardian must sign)

Mail to the **Reader Service:**
IN U.S.A.: P.O. Box 1867, Buffalo, NY 14240-1867
IN CANADA: P.O. Box 609, Fort Erie, Ontario L2A 5X3

Not valid for current subscribers to Harlequin Romantic Suspense books.

Want to try two free books from another line?
Call 1-800-873-8635 or visit www.ReaderService.com.

* Terms and prices subject to change without notice. Prices do not include applicable taxes. Sales tax applicable in N.Y. Canadian residents will be charged applicable taxes. Offer not valid in Quebec. This offer is limited to one order per household. All orders subject to credit approval. Credit or debit balances in a customer's account(s) may be offset by any other outstanding balance owed by or to the customer. Please allow 4 to 6 weeks for delivery. Offer available while quantities last.

Your Privacy—The Reader Service is committed to protecting your privacy. Our Privacy Policy is available online at www.ReaderService.com or upon request from the Reader Service.

We make a portion of our mailing list available to reputable third parties that offer products we believe may interest you. If you prefer that we not exchange your name with third parties, or if you wish to clarify or modify your communication preferences, please visit us at www.ReaderService.com/consumerschoice or write to us at Reader Service Preference Service, P.O. Box 9062, Buffalo, NY 14269. Include your complete name and address.

HRS11B

*Something's going on in Conard County's high school...
and Cassie Greaves has just landed in the middle of it.*

Take a sneak peek at RANCHER'S DEADLY RISK
by New York Times *bestselling author Rachel Lee, coming
in November 2012 from Harlequin® Romantic Suspense.*

"There comes a point, Cassie, when you've got to realize that stuff you got away with as a child is no longer acceptable or even legal."

Linc paused, realizing he must seem to be going around in circles. Well, he probably was, between her damned scent and his own uncertainty about what was happening.

"I'll be honest with you," he said slowly. "I'm wondering what's been bubbling beneath the surface at the school that I'm not aware of. That makes me uneasy. On the one hand, I'm trying to paint it in the best light because I know these kids. Or thought I did. I don't want to think the worst of any of them. On the other hand, I guess I shouldn't make too light of it. There have been three transgressions we know about with you. Four, if we add James. I'm not going to dismiss it, but I'm not going to be Chicken Little yet, either. The mind of a teenage male is impenetrable."

She surprised him by losing her haunted look and actually laughing. "You're right, it is. And girls aren't much better at that age."

Girls weren't much better at any age, he thought a little while later as he drove her home. He'd certainly never figured them out.

"Thanks for a wonderful time," she said as he walked her to her door. "I really enjoyed it."

"So did I," he answered more truthfully than he would have liked. He had to bite his tongue to keep from suggesting they do it again.

She was still smiling as she said good-night and closed the door.

He walked back to his truck, keys jingling in his hand, and thought about it all, from the bullying to the rat to the evening just past. The thoughts were still rumbling around when he got home.

Something wasn't right. Something. He'd grown up here, gone to school here, been away only during his college years, and now had been teaching for a decade.

His nose was telling him something was wrong. Very wrong. The question was what. And who.

Find out more in RANCHER'S DEADLY RISK
by Rachel Lee, available November 2012
from Harlequin® Romantic Suspense.